DreamWorks

DRAGONS
RIDERS OF BERK

VOLUME FOUR

THE STOWAWAY

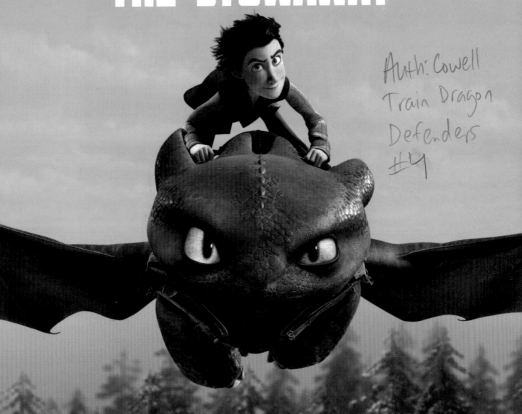

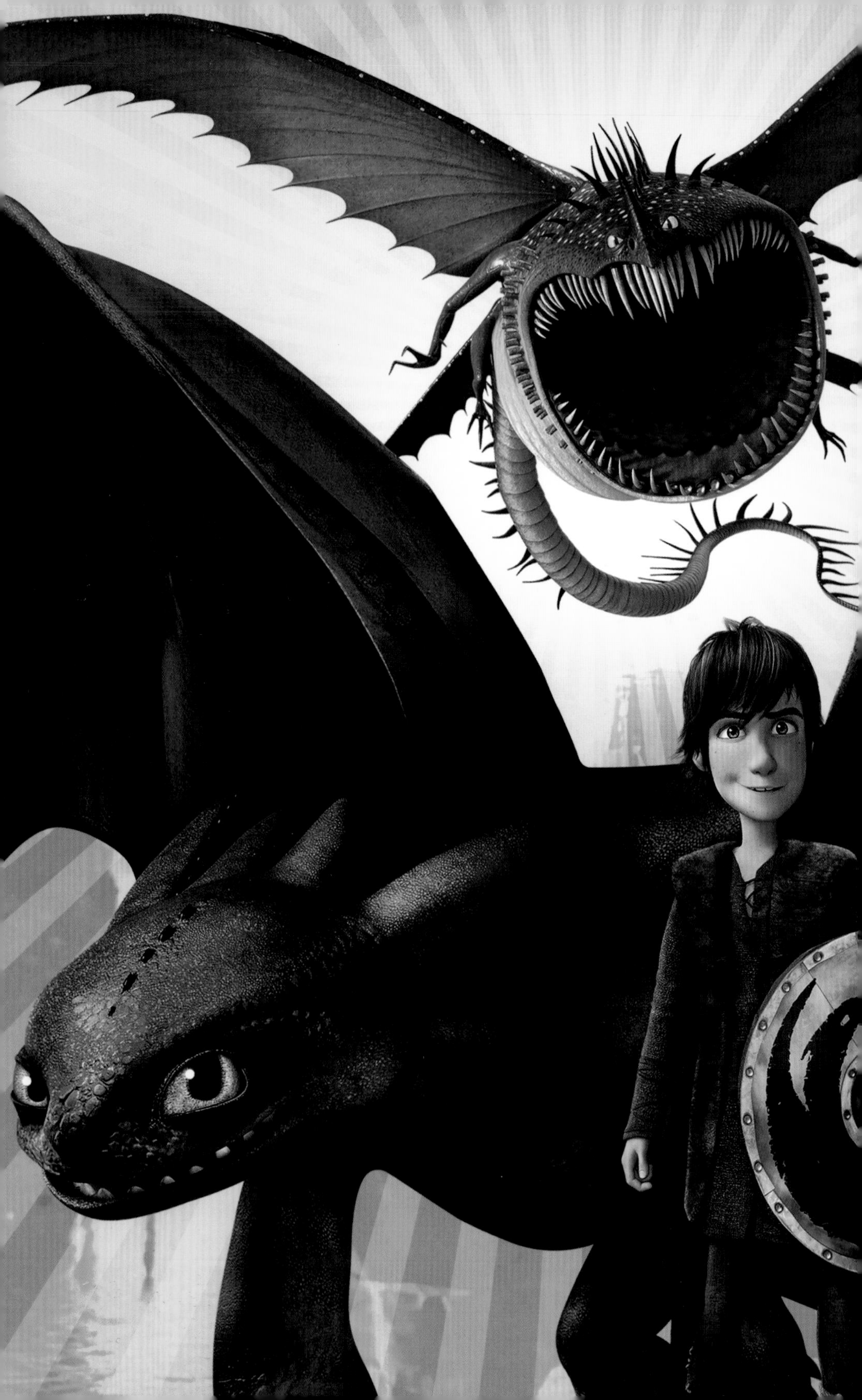

DREAMWORKS
DRAGONS
RIDERS OF BERK

VOLUME FOUR

THE STOWAWAY

SCRIPT
SIMON FURMAN

PENCILS & INKS
IWAN NAZIF

COLORING
DIGIKORE

LETTERING
JIM CAMPBELL

EDITOR
MARTIN EDEN

TITAN
COMICS

DreamWorks
DRAGONS
RIDERS OF BERK

WELCOME TO BERK, THE HOME OF HICCUP AND HIS DRAGON, TOOTHLESS, PLUS HICCUP'S FRIENDS WHO TRAIN AT THE DRAGON TRAINING ACADEMY!

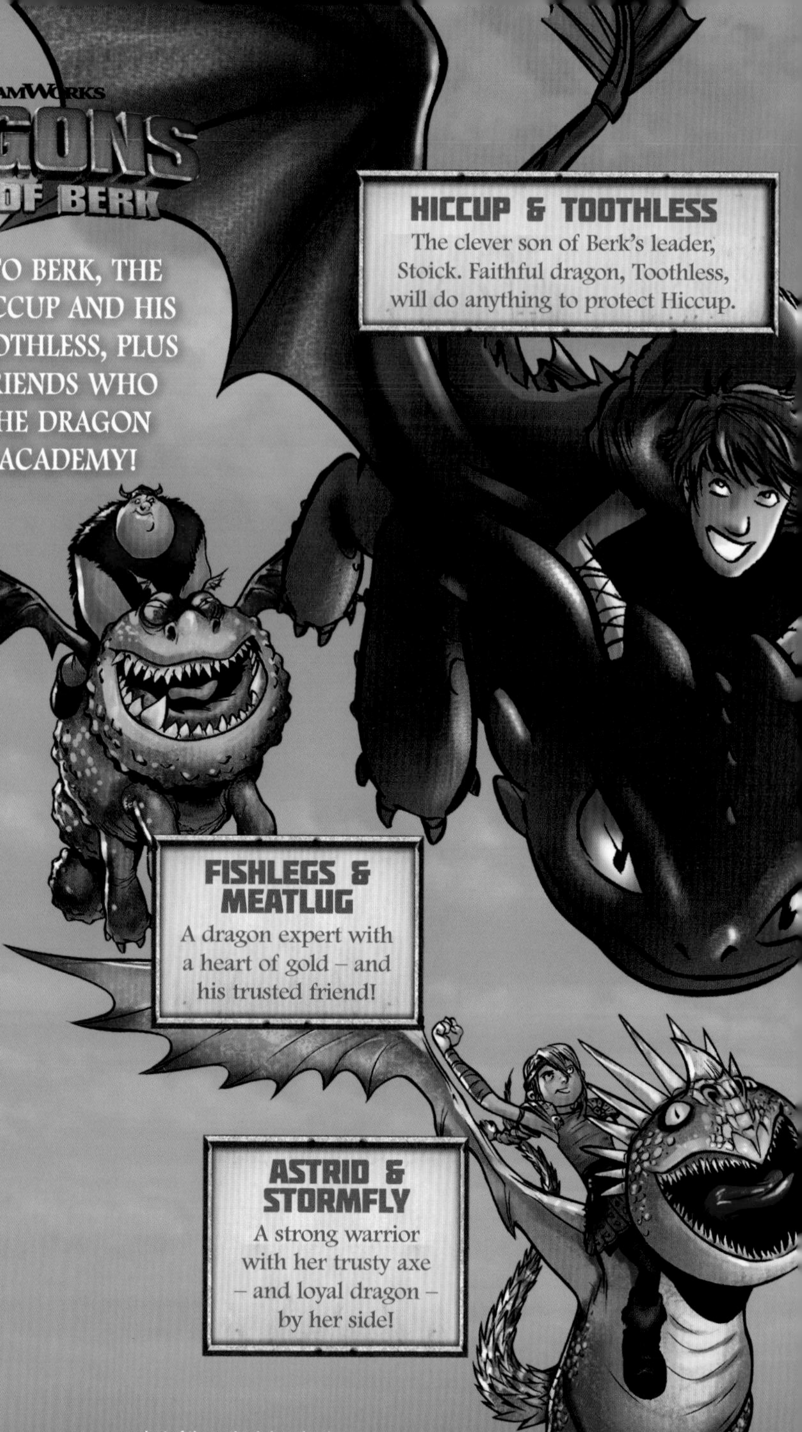
HICCUP & TOOTHLESS
The clever son of Berk's leader, Stoick. Faithful dragon, Toothless, will do anything to protect Hiccup.
FISHLEGS & MEATLUG
A dragon expert with a heart of gold – and his trusted friend!
ASTRID & STORMFLY
A strong warrior with her trusty axe – and loyal dragon – by her side!

TITAN EDITORIAL

Senior Editor
MARTIN EDEN

Production Manager
OBI ONOURA

Production Supervisors
PETER JAMES, JACKIE FLOOK

Studio Manager
EMMA SMITH

Circulation Manager
STEVE TOTHILL

Marketing Manager
RICKY CLAYDON

Publishing Manager
DARRYL TOTHILL

Publishing Director
CHRIS TEATHER

Operations Director
LEIGH BAULCH

Executive Director
VIVIAN CHEUNG

Publisher
NICK LANDAU

ISBN: 9781782760795

Published by Titan Comics, a division of Titan Publishing Group Ltd. 144 Southwark St. London, SE1 0UP

10 9 8 7 6 5 4 3 2 1

First printed in China in March 2015.

A CIP catalogue record for this title is available from the British Library.

Titan Comics. TC0161

Special thanks to Corinne Combs, Alyssa Mauney, Barbara Layman, and Andre Siregar.

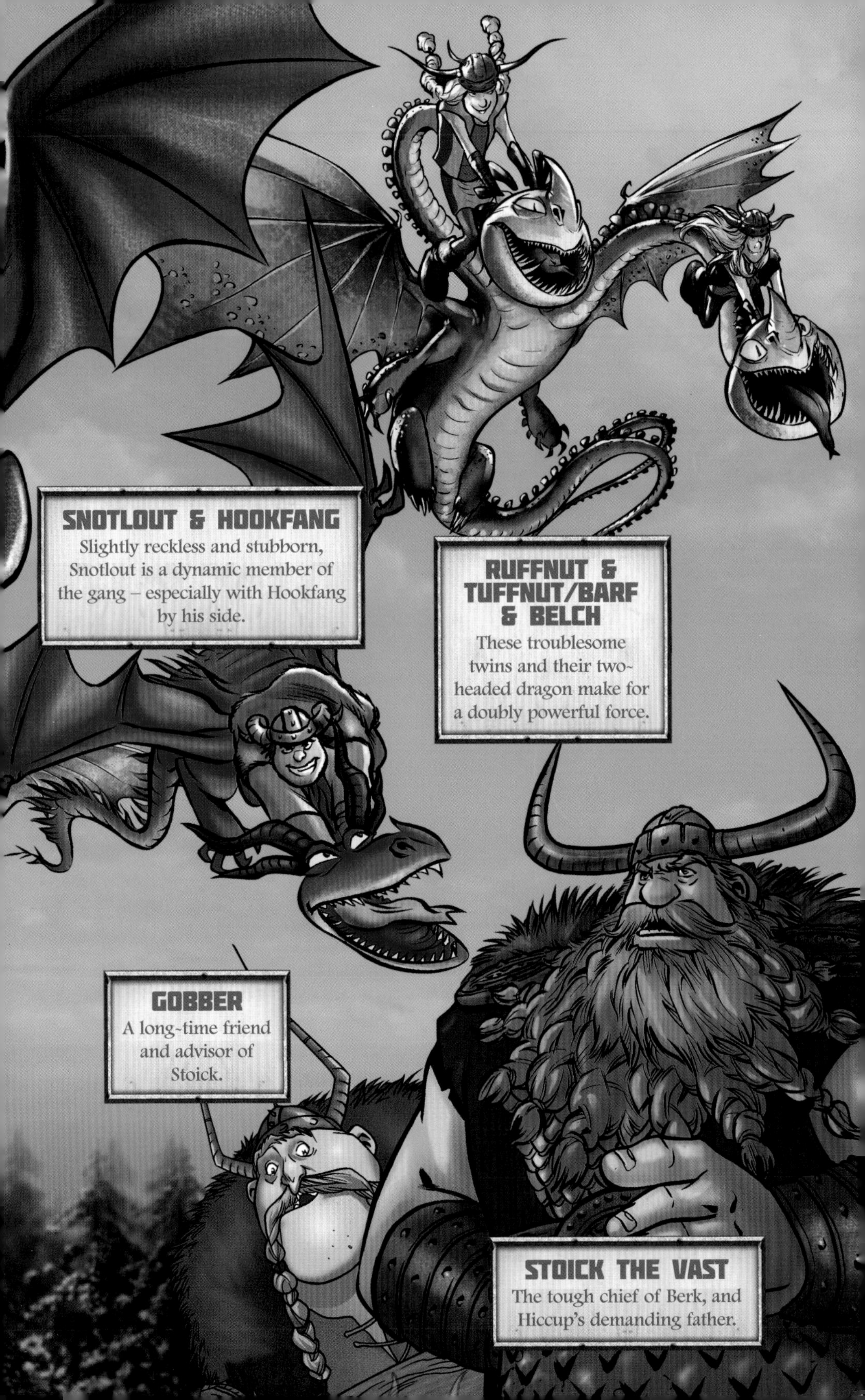
SNOTLOUT & HOOKFANG
Slightly reckless and stubborn, Snotlout is a dynamic member of the gang – especially with Hookfang by his side.
RUFFNUT & TUFFNUT/BARF & BELCH
These troublesome twins and their two-headed dragon make for a doubly powerful force.
GOBBER
A long-time friend and advisor of Stoick.
STOICK THE VAST
The tough chief of Berk, and Hiccup's demanding father.

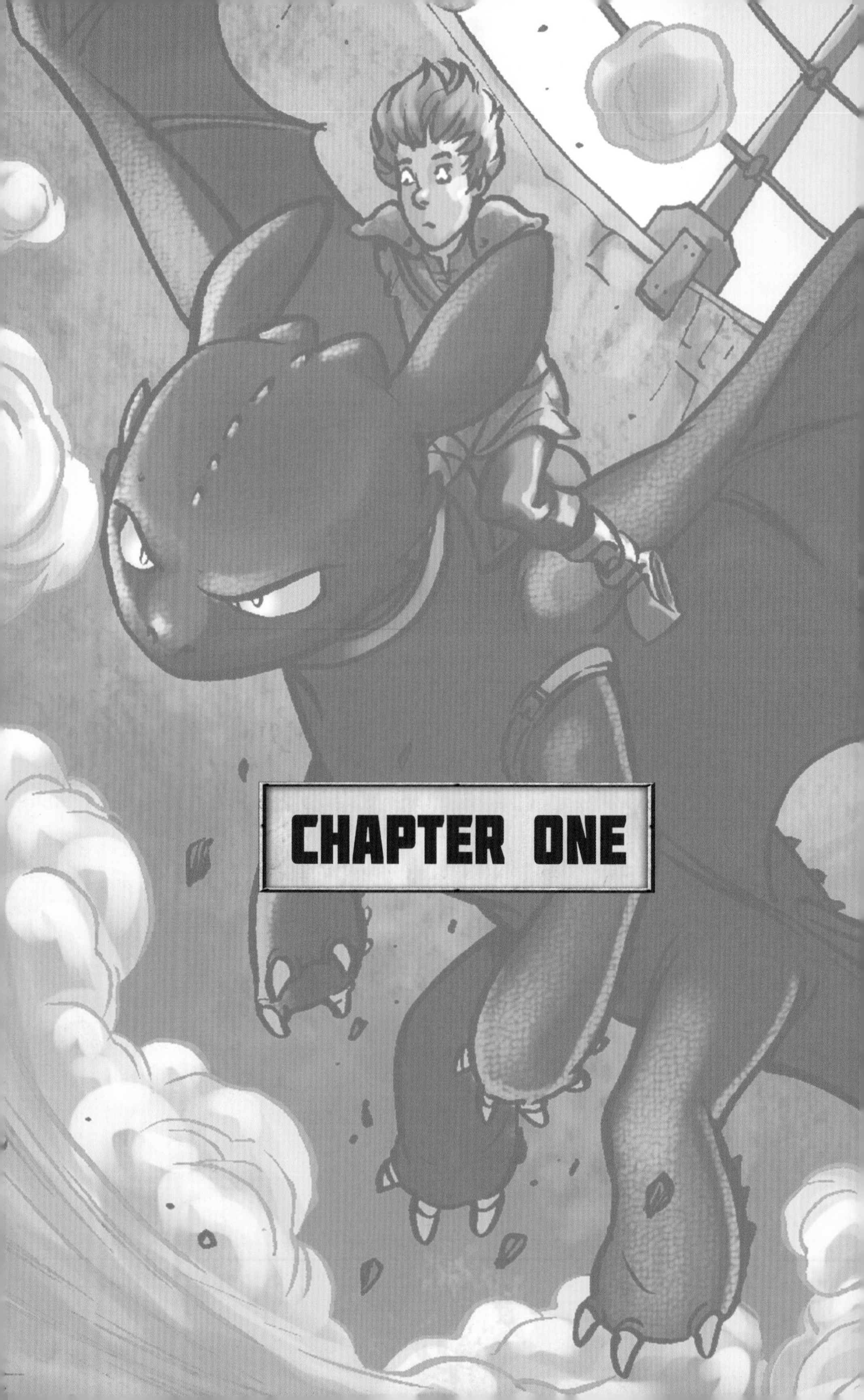

CHAPTER ONE

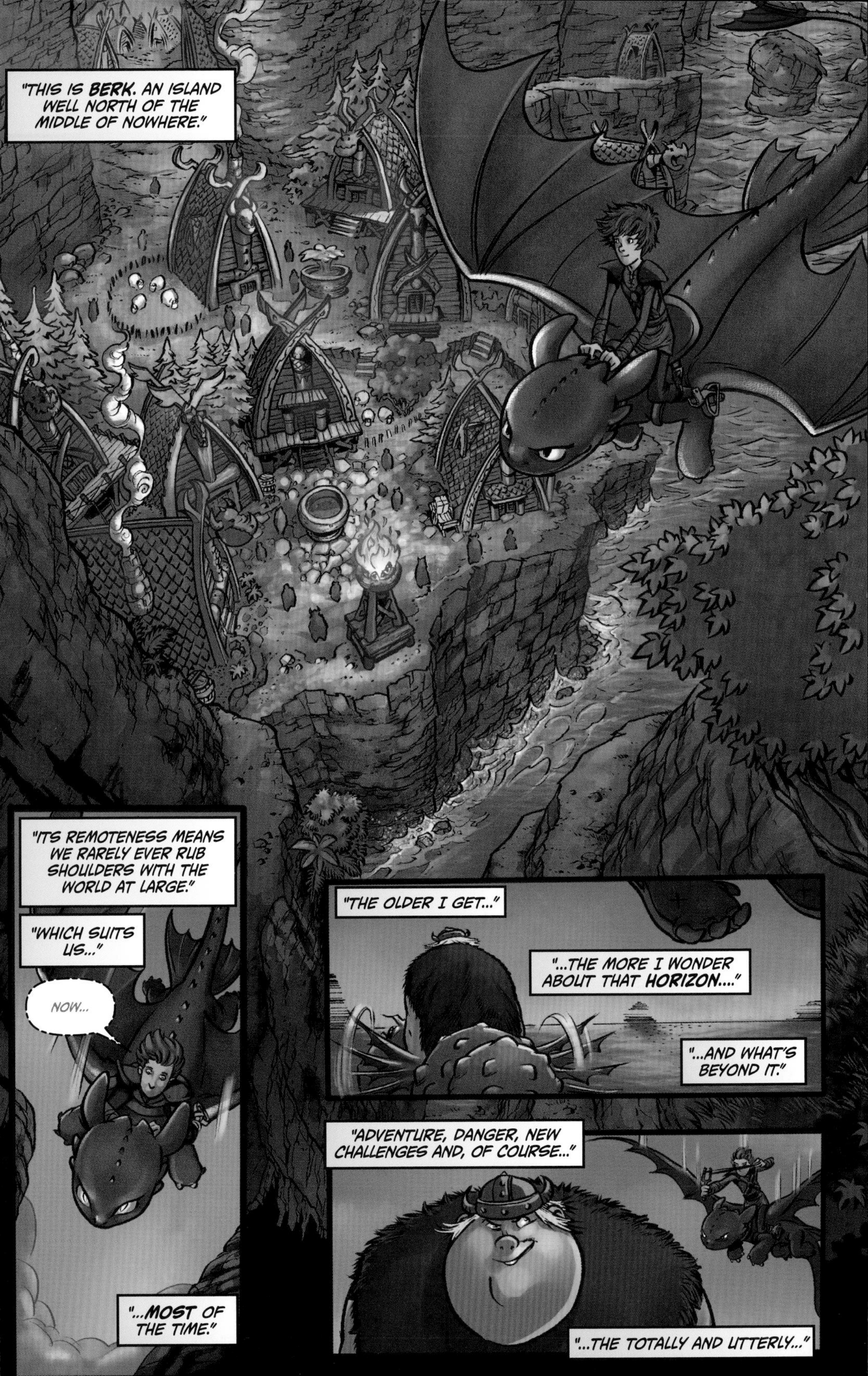
"THIS IS BERK. AN ISLAND WELL NORTH OF THE MIDDLE OF NOWHERE."
"ITS REMOTENESS MEANS WE RARELY EVER RUB SHOULDERS WITH THE WORLD AT LARGE."
"WHICH SUITS US..."
NOW...
"...MOST OF THE TIME."
"THE OLDER I GET..."
"...THE MORE I WONDER ABOUT THAT HORIZON...."
"...AND WHAT'S BEYOND IT."
"ADVENTURE, DANGER, NEW CHALLENGES AND, OF COURSE..."
"...THE TOTALLY AND UTTERLY..."

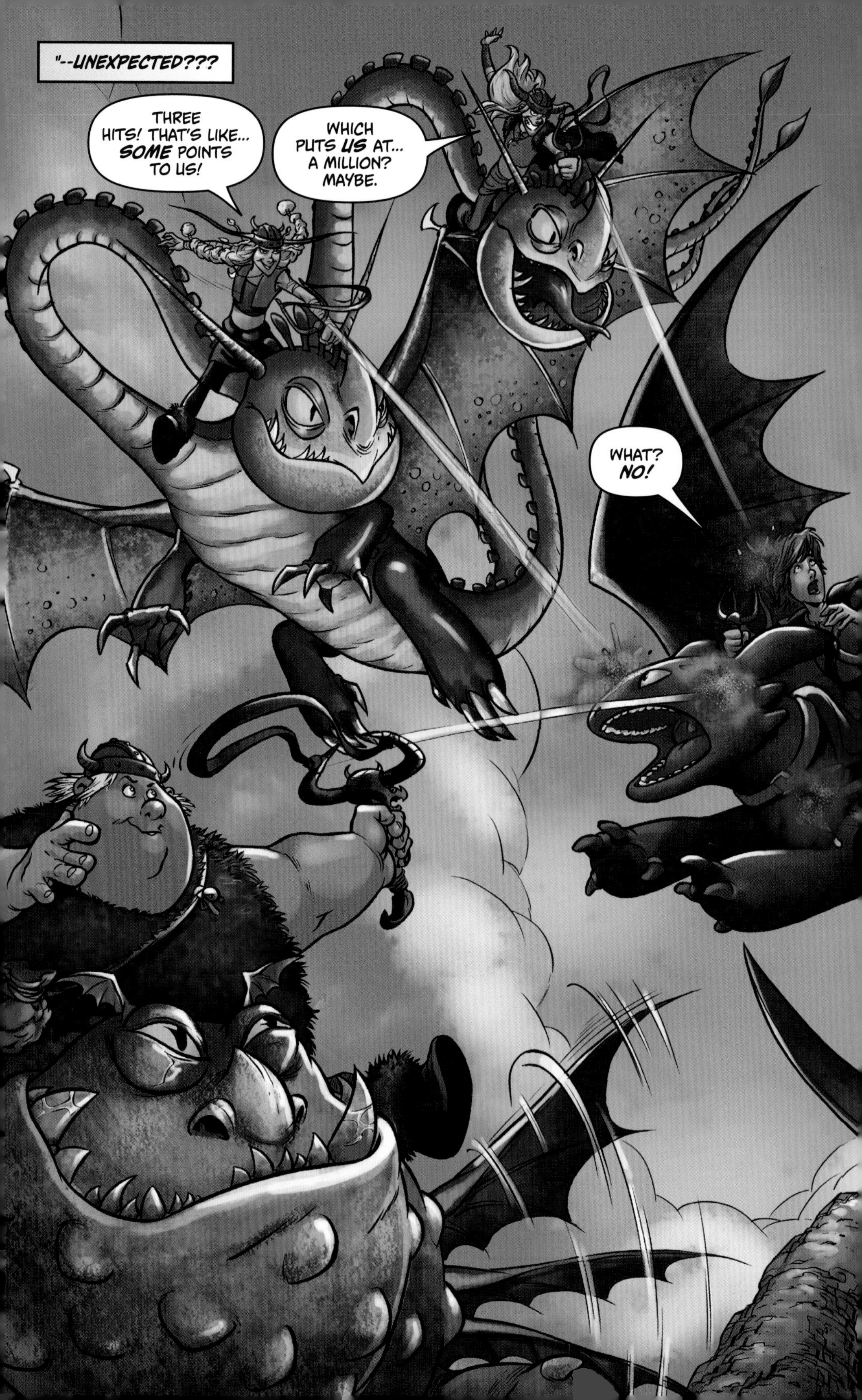
"--UNEXPECTED???
THREE HITS! THAT'S LIKE... SOME POINTS TO US!
WHICH PUTS US AT... A MILLION? MAYBE.
WHAT? NO!

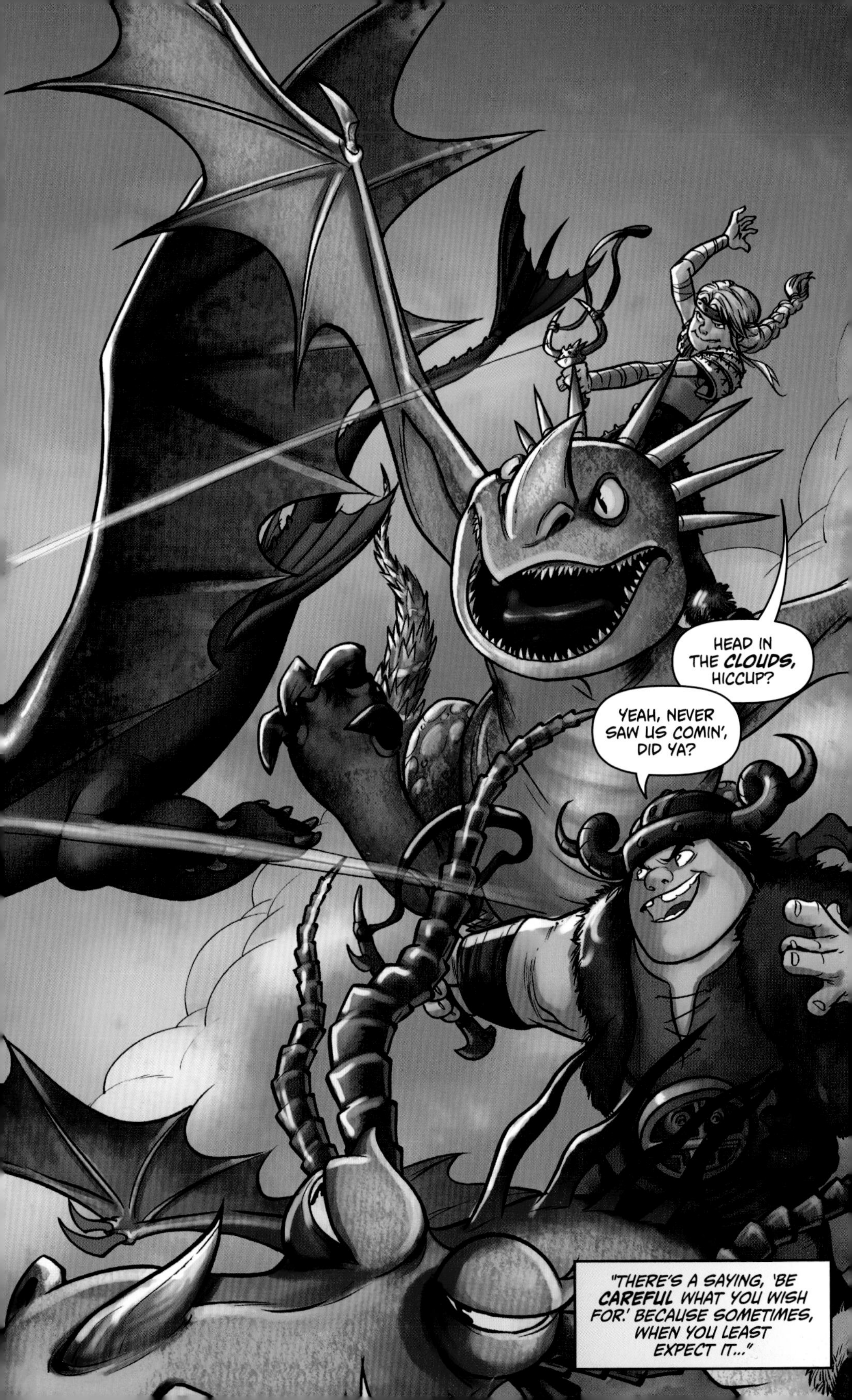
HEAD IN THE **CLOUDS,** HICCUP?
YEAH, NEVER SAW US COMIN', DID YA?
"THERE'S A SAYING, 'BE **CAREFUL** WHAT YOU WISH FOR.' BECAUSE SOMETIMES, WHEN YOU LEAST EXPECT IT..."

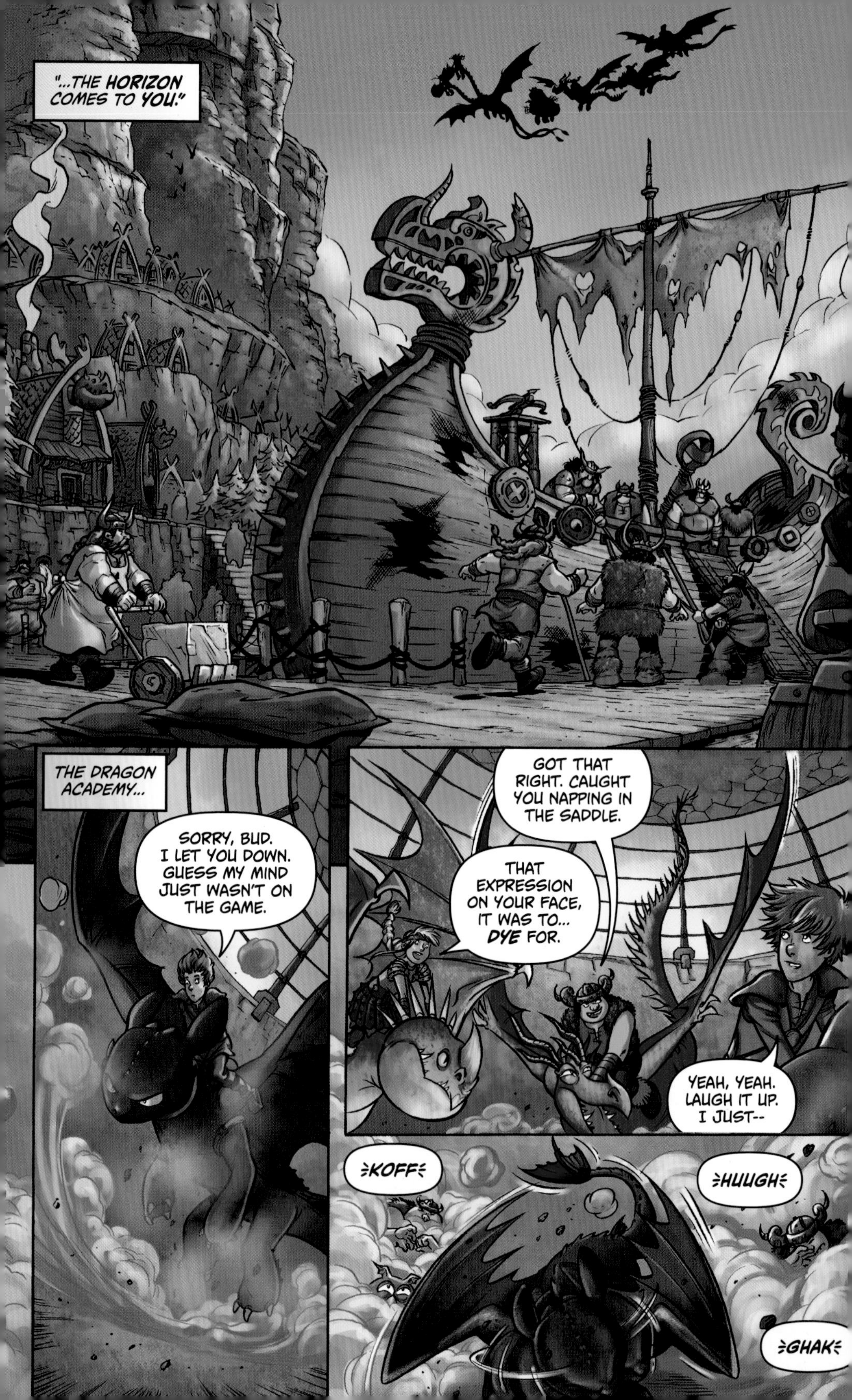
"...THE HORIZON COMES TO YOU."
THE DRAGON ACADEMY...
SORRY, BUD. I LET YOU DOWN. GUESS MY MIND JUST WASN'T ON THE GAME.
GOT THAT RIGHT. CAUGHT YOU NAPPING IN THE SADDLE.
THAT EXPRESSION ON YOUR FACE, IT WAS TO... DYE FOR.
YEAH, YEAH. LAUGH IT UP. I JUST--
KOFF
HUUGH
GHAK

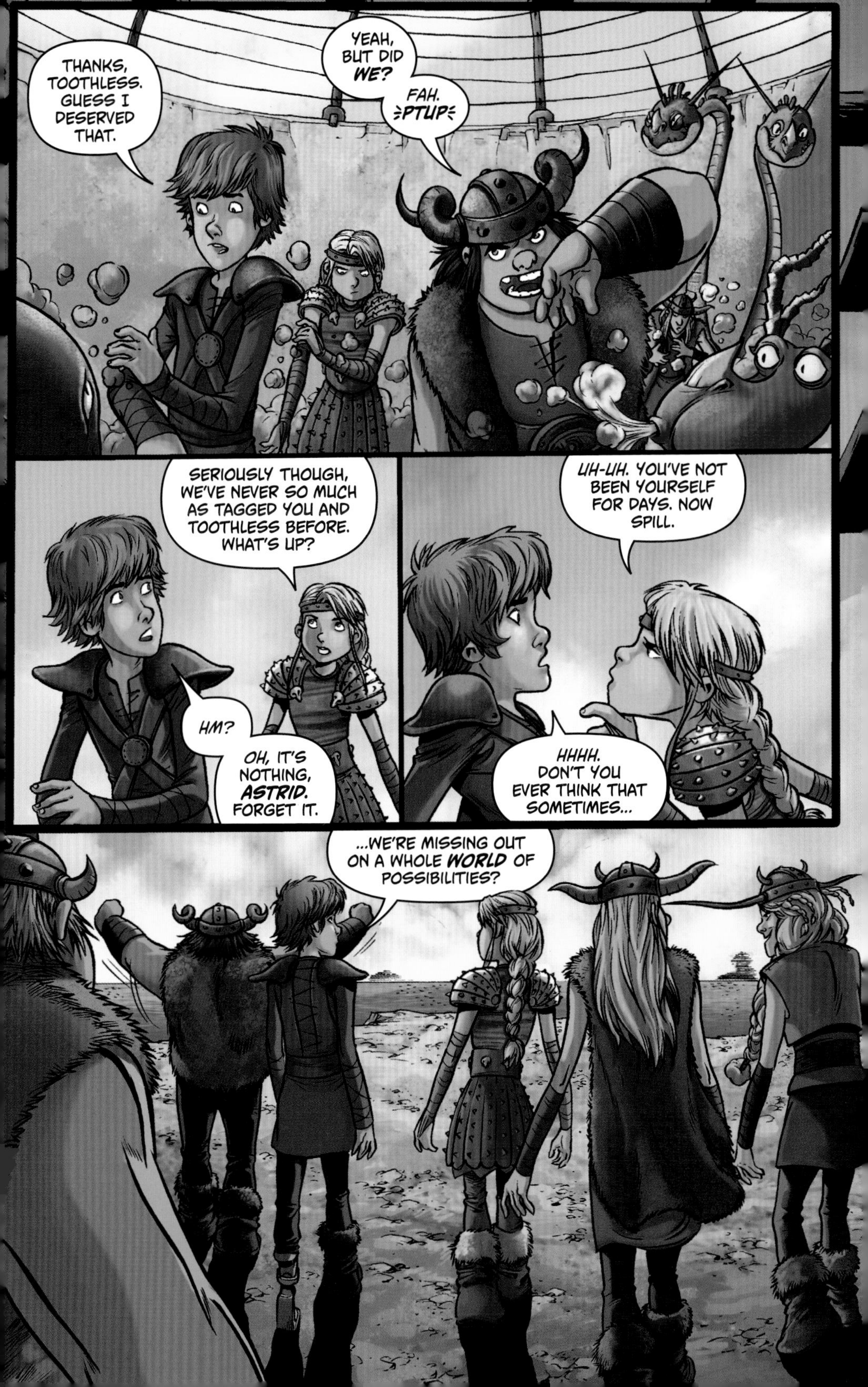
THANKS, TOOTHLESS. GUESS I DESERVED THAT.
YEAH, BUT DID WE?
FAH. PTUP
SERIOUSLY THOUGH, WE'VE NEVER SO MUCH AS TAGGED YOU AND TOOTHLESS BEFORE. WHAT'S UP?
HM?
OH, IT'S NOTHING, ASTRID. FORGET IT.
UH-UH. YOU'VE NOT BEEN YOURSELF FOR DAYS. NOW SPILL.
HHHH. DON'T YOU EVER THINK THAT SOMETIMES...
...WE'RE MISSING OUT ON A WHOLE WORLD OF POSSIBILITIES?

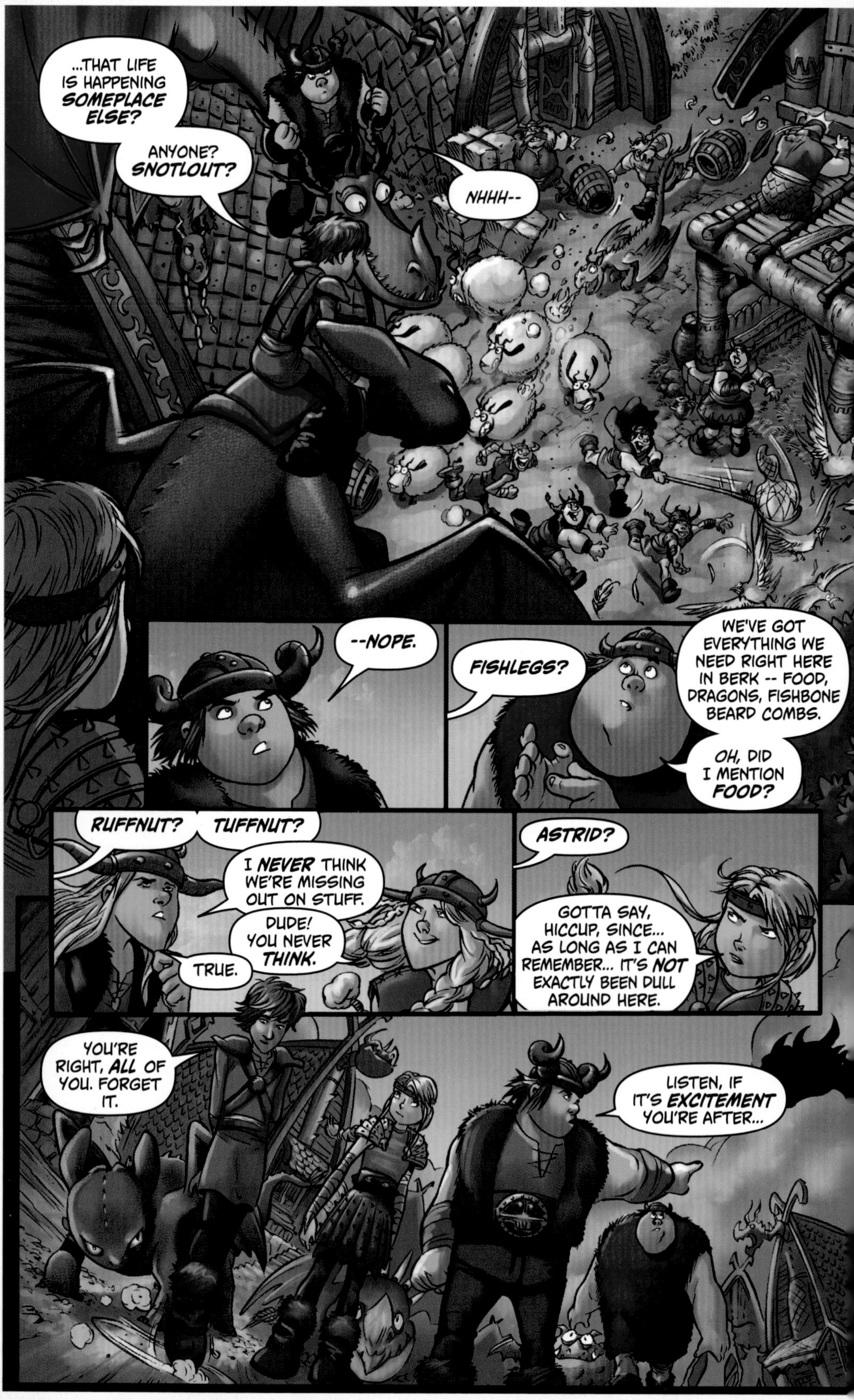
...THAT LIFE IS HAPPENING SOMEPLACE ELSE?
ANYONE? SNOTLOUT?
NHHH--
--NOPE.
FISHLEGS?
WE'VE GOT EVERYTHING WE NEED RIGHT HERE IN BERK -- FOOD, DRAGONS, FISHBONE BEARD COMBS.
OH, DID I MENTION FOOD?
RUFFNUT?
TUFFNUT?
I NEVER THINK WE'RE MISSING OUT ON STUFF.
DUDE! YOU NEVER THINK.
TRUE.
ASTRID?
GOTTA SAY, HICCUP, SINCE... AS LONG AS I CAN REMEMBER... IT'S NOT EXACTLY BEEN DULL AROUND HERE.
YOU'RE RIGHT, ALL OF YOU. FORGET IT.
LISTEN, IF IT'S EXCITEMENT YOU'RE AFTER...

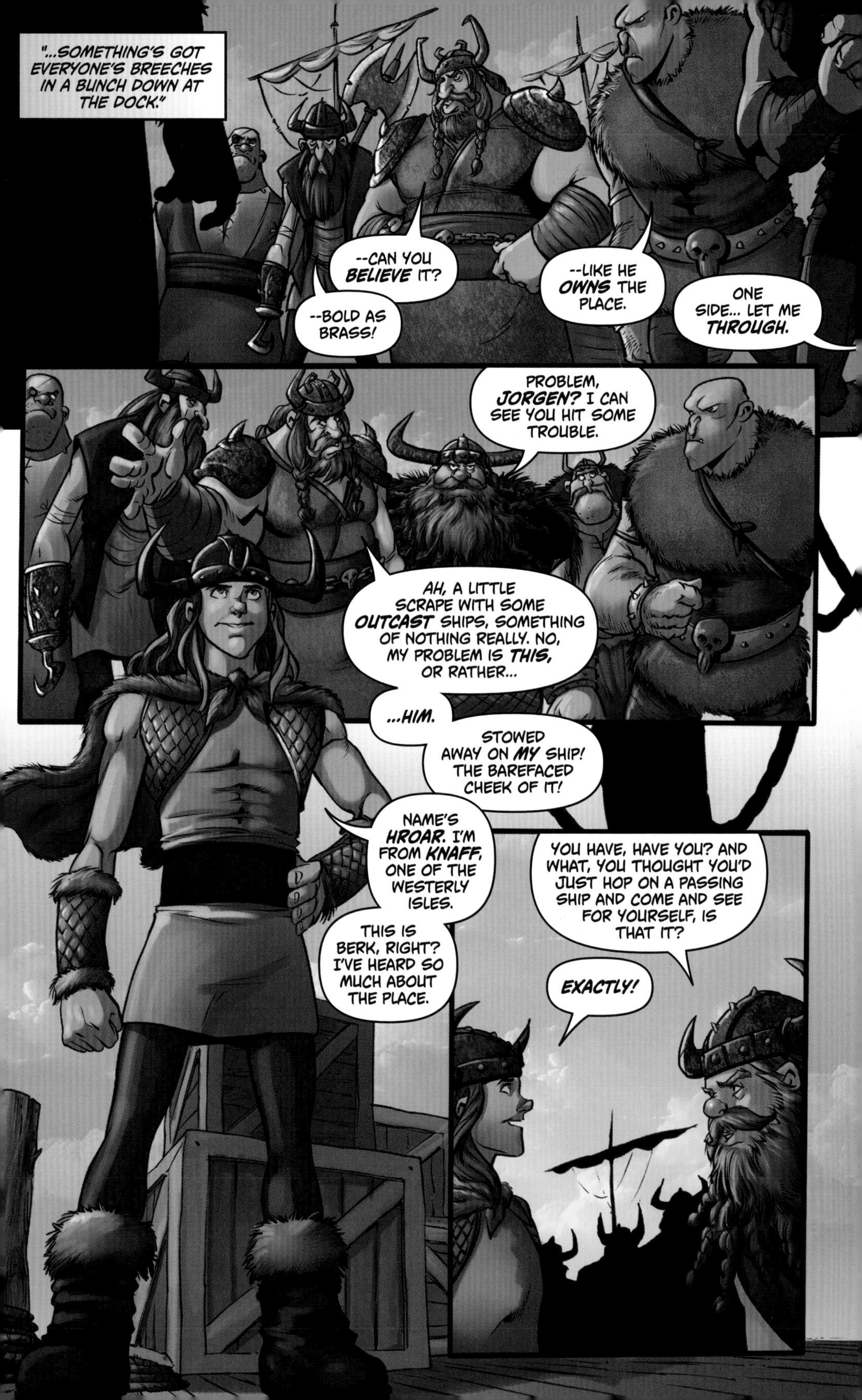
"...SOMETHING'S GOT EVERYONE'S BREECHES IN A BUNCH DOWN AT THE DOCK."
--CAN YOU BELIEVE IT?
--BOLD AS BRASS!
--LIKE HE OWNS THE PLACE.
ONE SIDE... LET ME THROUGH.
PROBLEM, JORGEN? I CAN SEE YOU HIT SOME TROUBLE.
AH, A LITTLE SCRAPE WITH SOME OUTCAST SHIPS, SOMETHING OF NOTHING REALLY. NO, MY PROBLEM IS THIS, OR RATHER...
...HIM.
STOWED AWAY ON MY SHIP! THE BAREFACED CHEEK OF IT!
NAME'S HROAR. I'M FROM KNAFF, ONE OF THE WESTERLY ISLES.
THIS IS BERK, RIGHT? I'VE HEARD SO MUCH ABOUT THE PLACE.
YOU HAVE, HAVE YOU? AND WHAT, YOU THOUGHT YOU'D JUST HOP ON A PASSING SHIP AND COME AND SEE FOR YOURSELF, IS THAT IT?
EXACTLY!

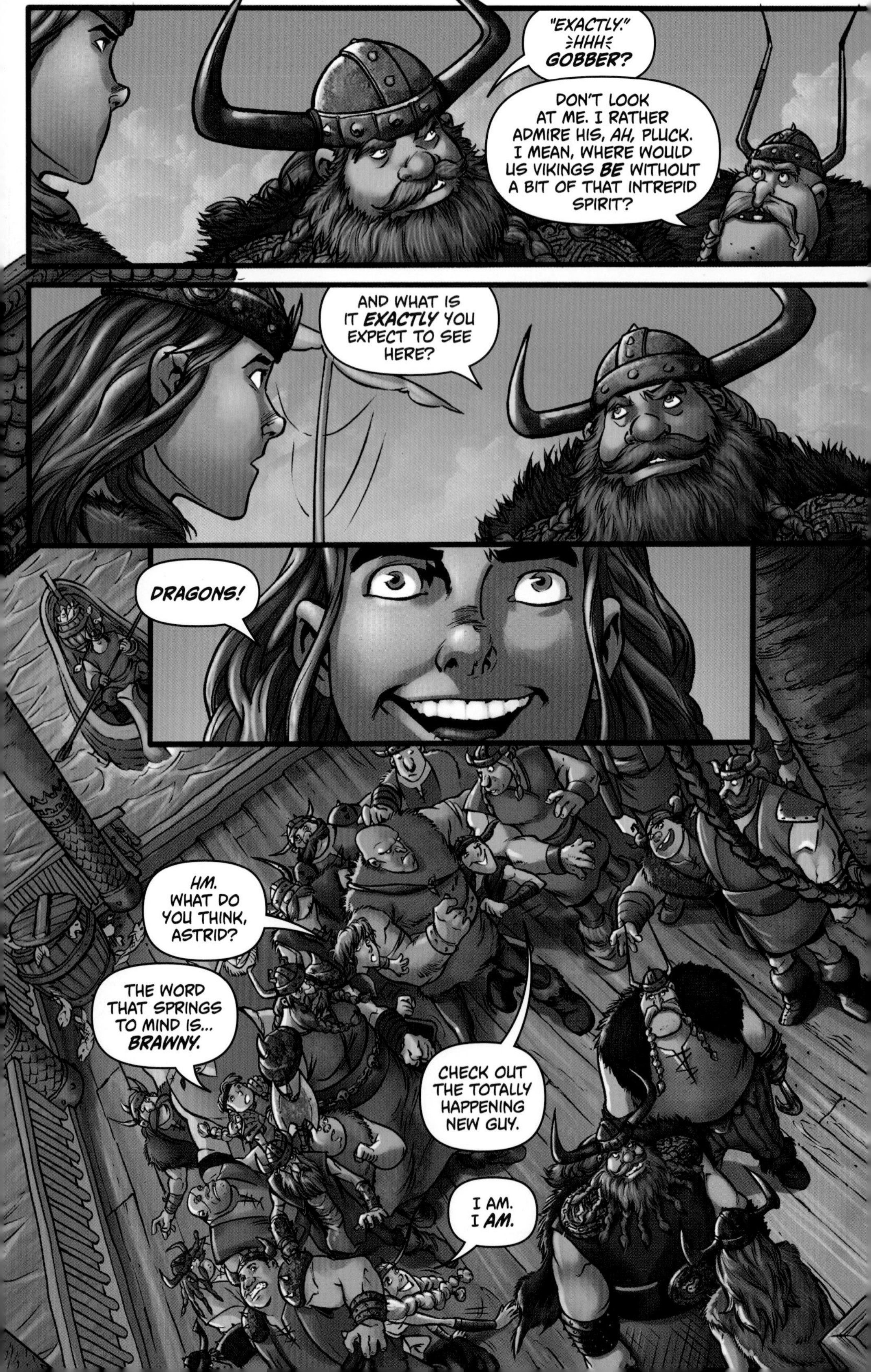
"EXACTLY." ≷HHH≶ GOBBER?
DON'T LOOK AT ME. I RATHER ADMIRE HIS, AH, PLUCK. I MEAN, WHERE WOULD US VIKINGS BE WITHOUT A BIT OF THAT INTREPID SPIRIT?
AND WHAT IS IT EXACTLY YOU EXPECT TO SEE HERE?
DRAGONS!
HM. WHAT DO YOU THINK, ASTRID?
THE WORD THAT SPRINGS TO MIND IS... BRAWNY.
CHECK OUT THE TOTALLY HAPPENING NEW GUY.
I AM. I AM.

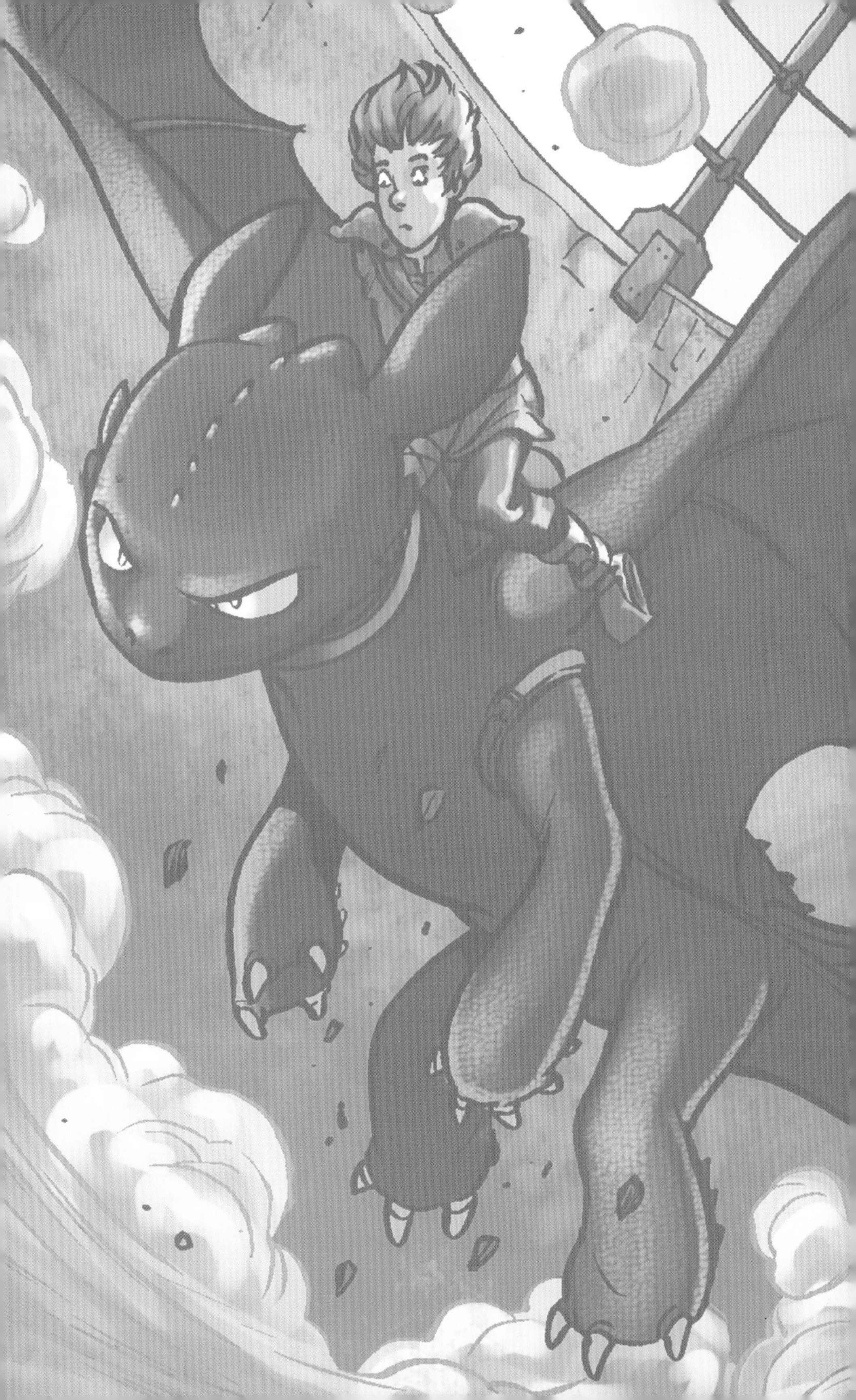

CHAPTER TWO

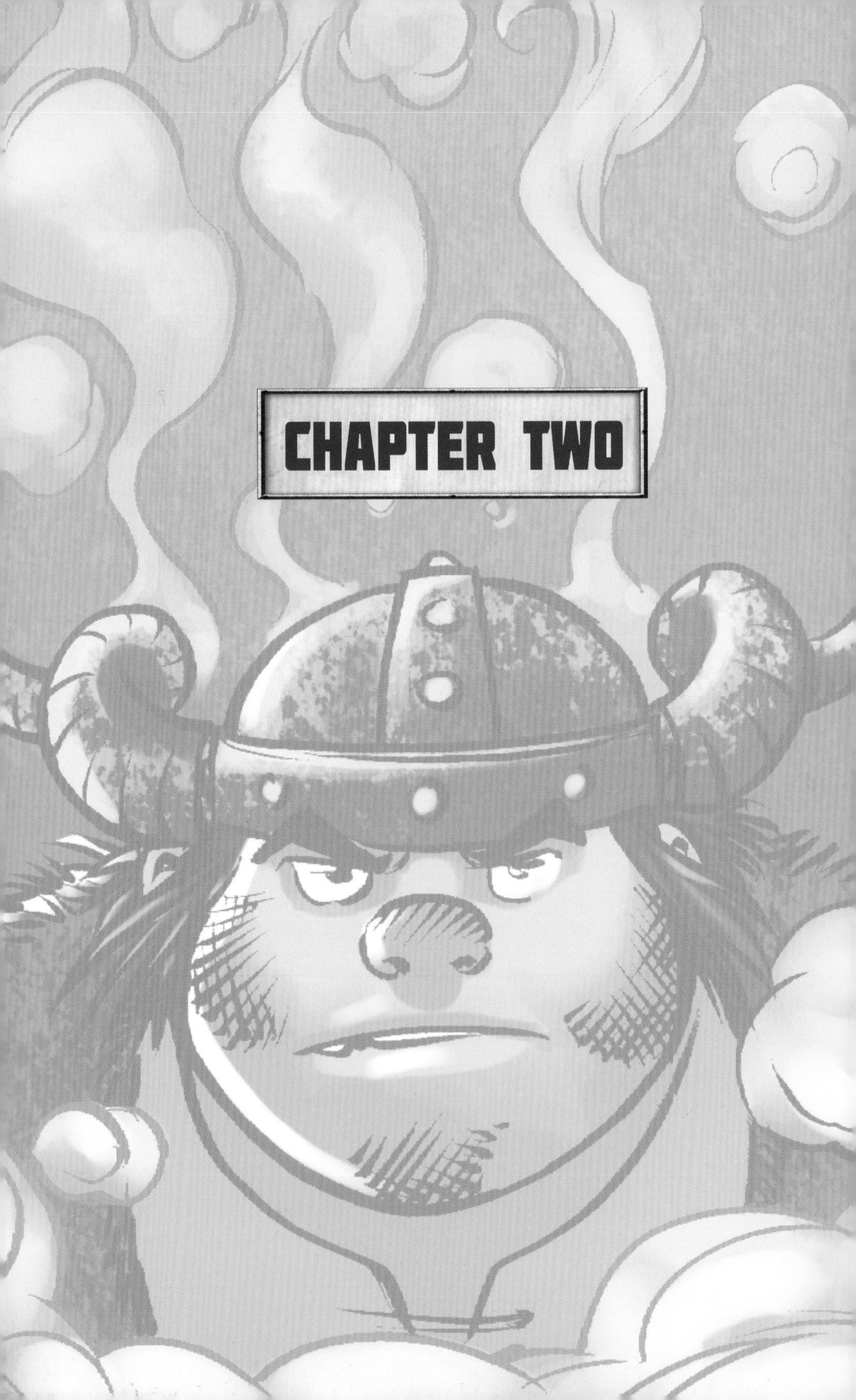

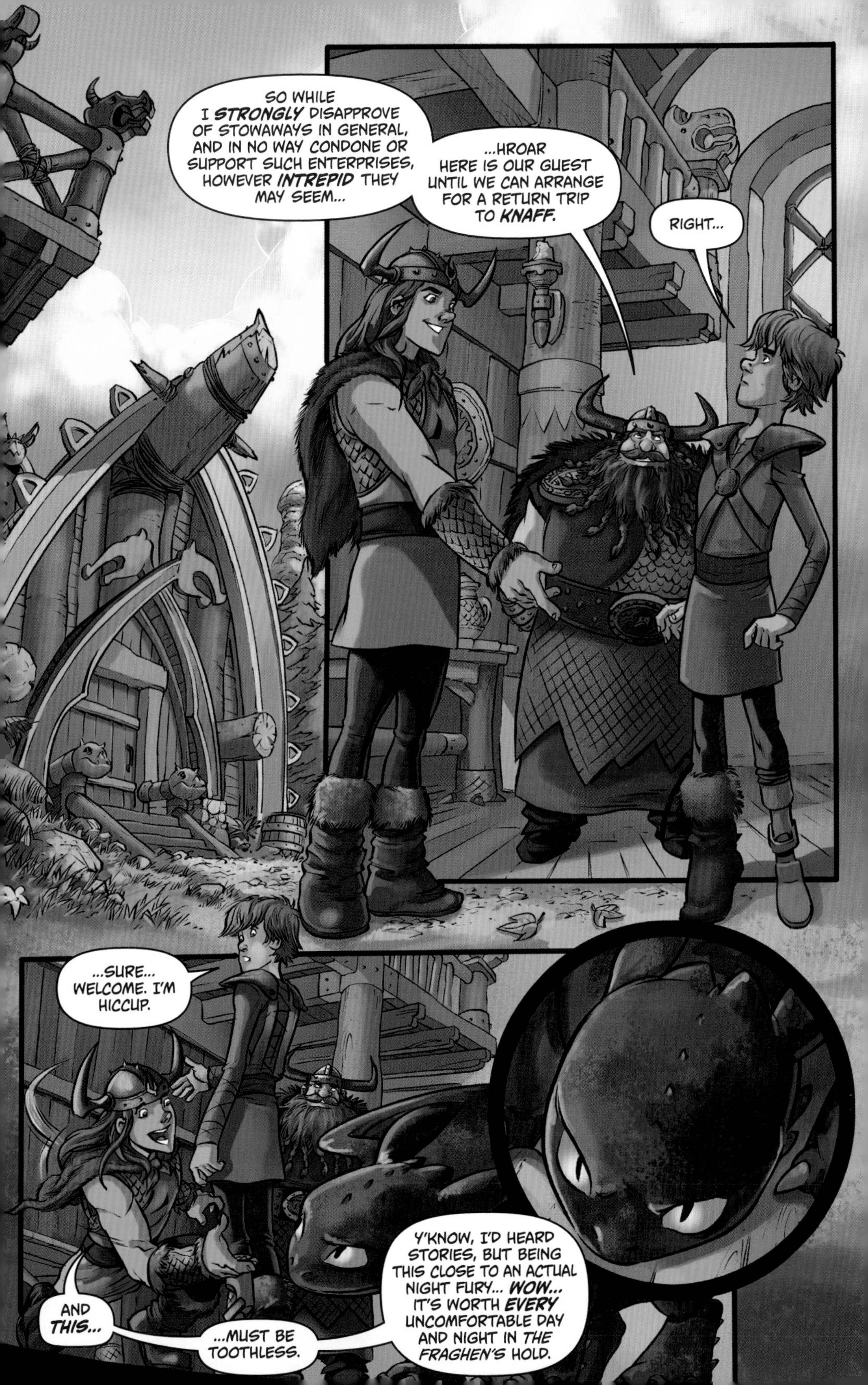
SO WHILE I **STRONGLY** DISAPPROVE OF STOWAWAYS IN GENERAL, AND IN NO WAY CONDONE OR SUPPORT SUCH ENTERPRISES, HOWEVER **INTREPID** THEY MAY SEEM...
...HROAR HERE IS OUR GUEST UNTIL WE CAN ARRANGE FOR A RETURN TRIP TO **KNAFF**.
RIGHT...
...SURE... WELCOME. I'M HICCUP.
AND **THIS...**
...MUST BE TOOTHLESS.
Y'KNOW, I'D HEARD STORIES, BUT BEING THIS CLOSE TO AN ACTUAL NIGHT FURY... **WOW...** IT'S WORTH **EVERY** UNCOMFORTABLE DAY AND NIGHT IN *THE FRAGHEN'S* HOLD.

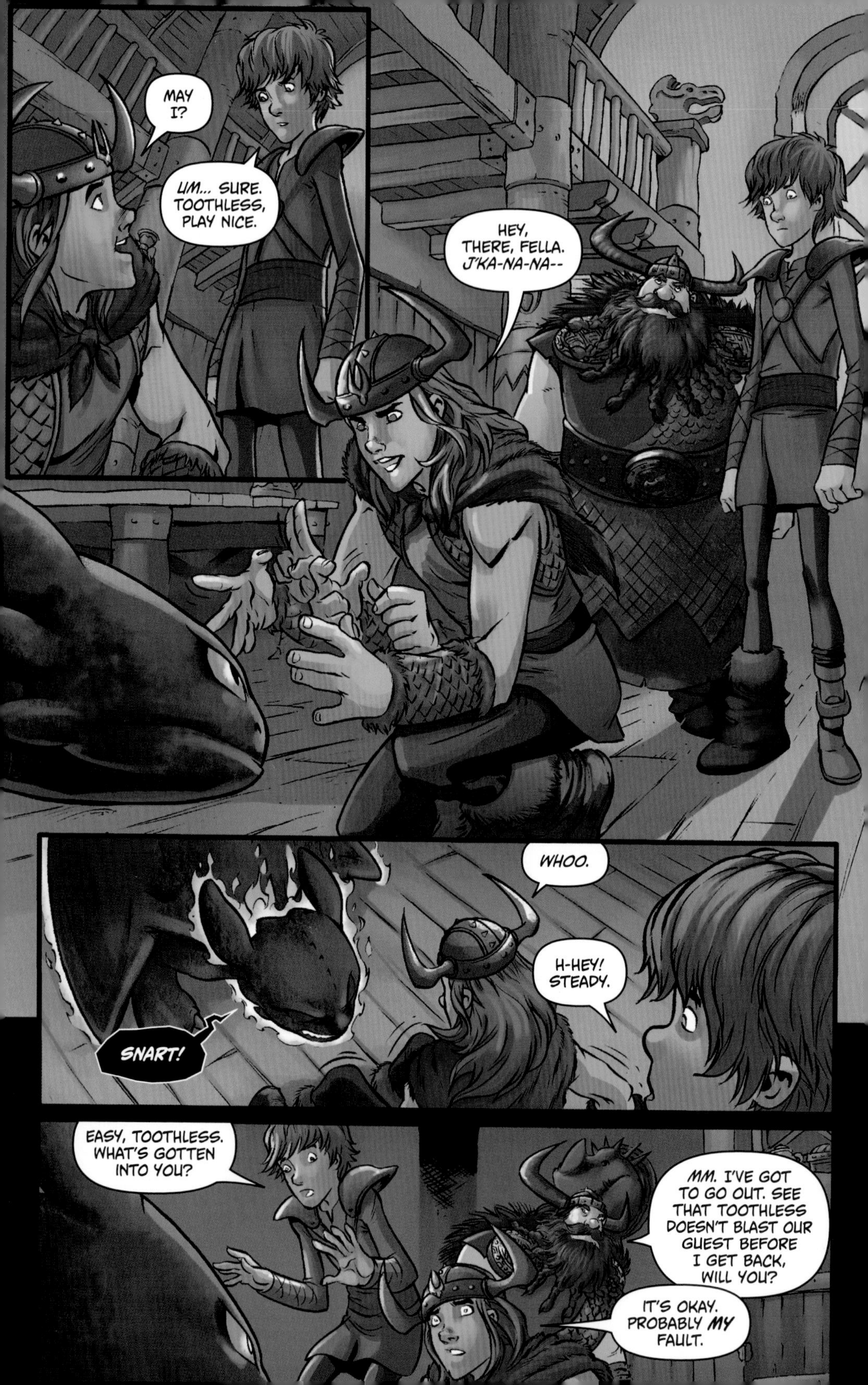
MAY I?
UM... SURE. TOOTHLESS, PLAY NICE.
HEY, THERE, FELLA. J'KA-NA-NA--
WHOO.
H-HEY! STEADY.
SNART!
EASY, TOOTHLESS. WHAT'S GOTTEN INTO YOU?
MM. I'VE GOT TO GO OUT. SEE THAT TOOTHLESS DOESN'T BLAST OUR GUEST BEFORE I GET BACK, WILL YOU?
IT'S OKAY. PROBABLY MY FAULT.

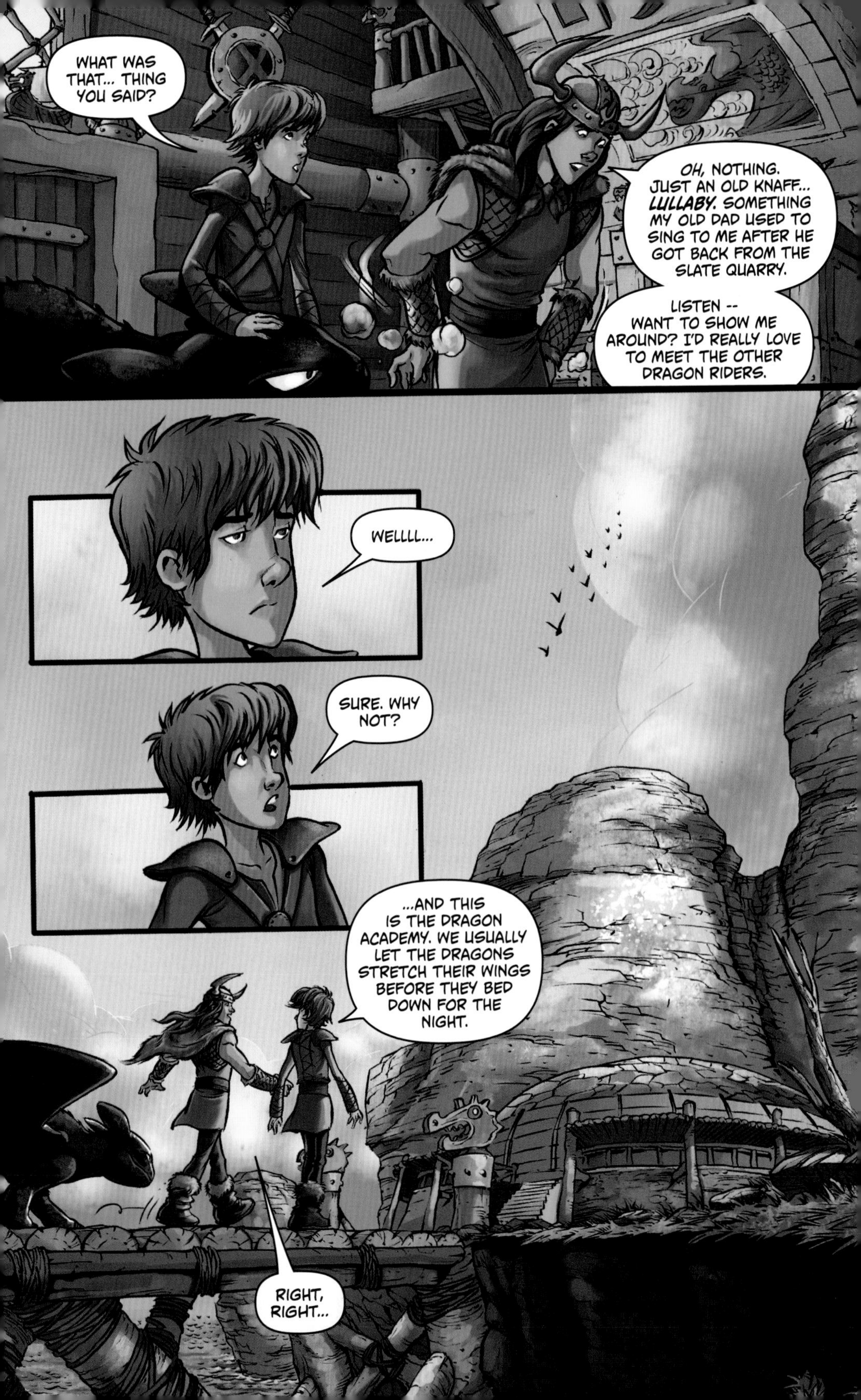
WHAT WAS THAT... THING YOU SAID?
OH, NOTHING. JUST AN OLD KNAFF... LULLABY. SOMETHING MY OLD DAD USED TO SING TO ME AFTER HE GOT BACK FROM THE SLATE QUARRY.
LISTEN -- WANT TO SHOW ME AROUND? I'D REALLY LOVE TO MEET THE OTHER DRAGON RIDERS.
WELLLL...
SURE. WHY NOT?
...AND THIS IS THE DRAGON ACADEMY. WE USUALLY LET THE DRAGONS STRETCH THEIR WINGS BEFORE THEY BED DOWN FOR THE NIGHT.
RIGHT, RIGHT...

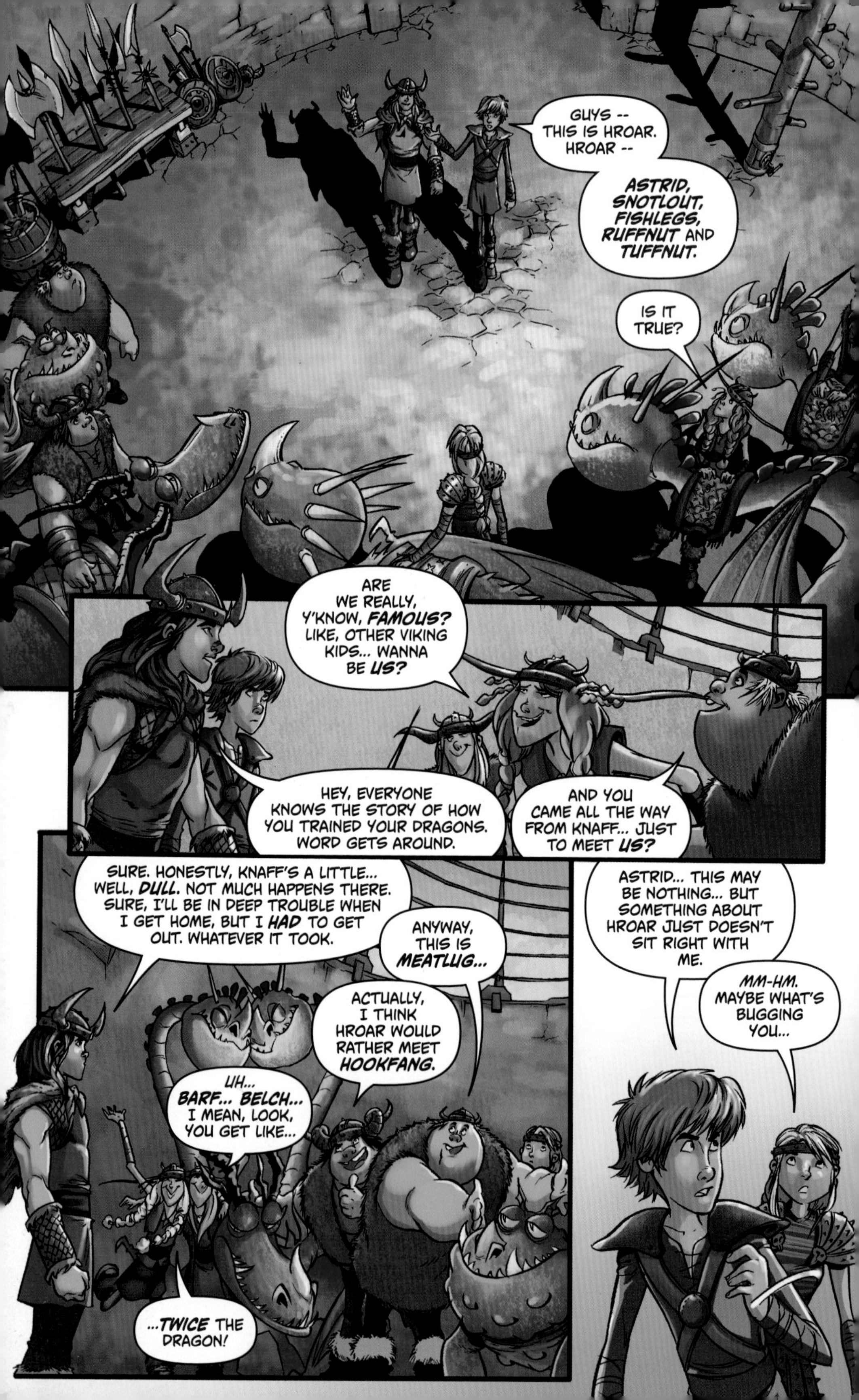
GUYS -- THIS IS HROAR. HROAR --
ASTRID, SNOTLOUT, FISHLEGS, RUFFNUT AND TUFFNUT.
IS IT TRUE?
ARE WE REALLY, Y'KNOW, FAMOUS? LIKE, OTHER VIKING KIDS... WANNA BE US?
HEY, EVERYONE KNOWS THE STORY OF HOW YOU TRAINED YOUR DRAGONS. WORD GETS AROUND.
AND YOU CAME ALL THE WAY FROM KNAFF... JUST TO MEET US?
SURE. HONESTLY, KNAFF'S A LITTLE... WELL, DULL. NOT MUCH HAPPENS THERE. SURE, I'LL BE IN DEEP TROUBLE WHEN I GET HOME, BUT I HAD TO GET OUT. WHATEVER IT TOOK.
ANYWAY, THIS IS MEATLUG...
ACTUALLY, I THINK HROAR WOULD RATHER MEET HOOKFANG.
UH... BARF... BELCH... I MEAN, LOOK, YOU GET LIKE...
...TWICE THE DRAGON!
ASTRID... THIS MAY BE NOTHING... BUT SOMETHING ABOUT HROAR JUST DOESN'T SIT RIGHT WITH ME.
MM-HM. MAYBE WHAT'S BUGGING YOU...

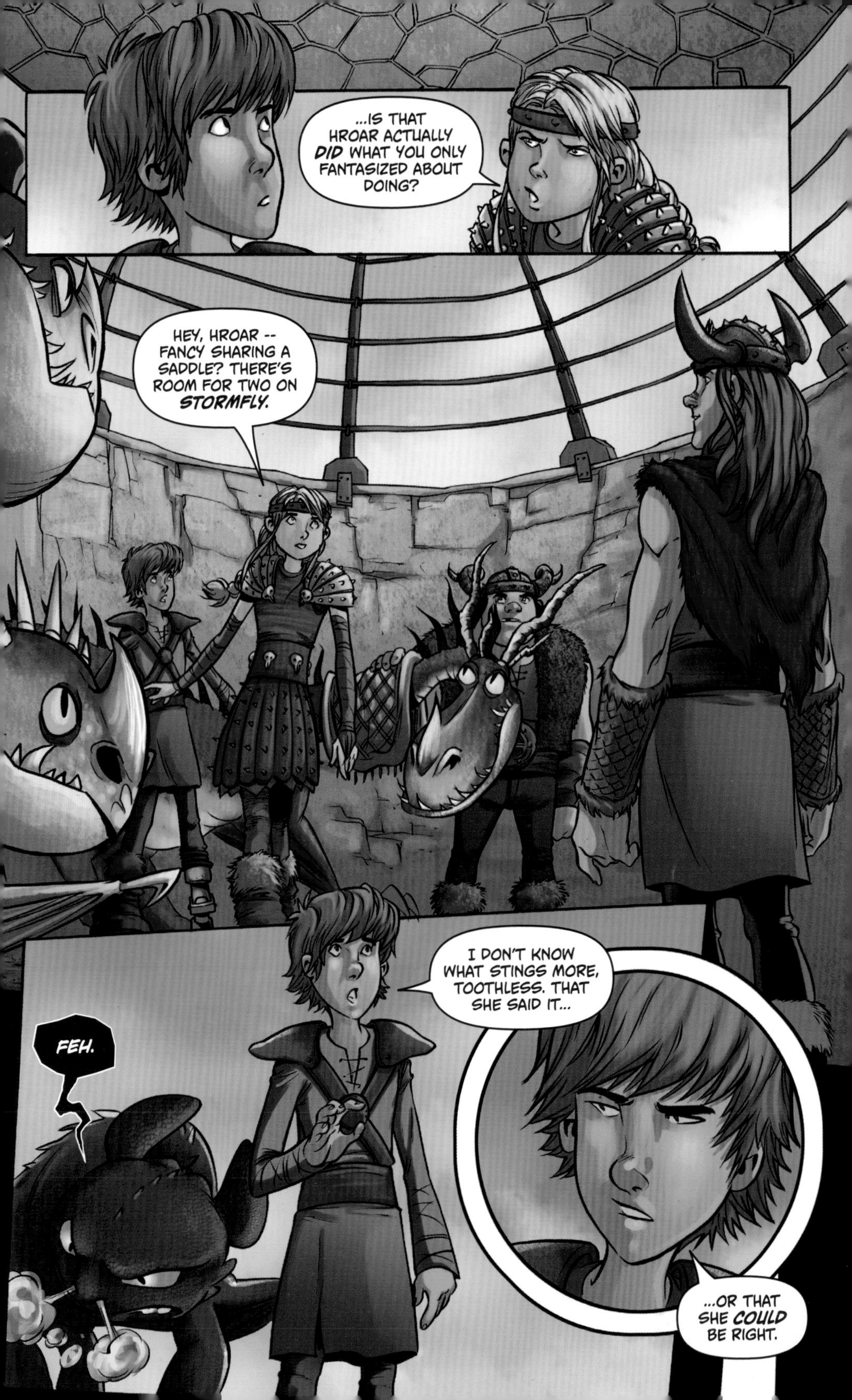
...IS THAT HROAR ACTUALLY DID WHAT YOU ONLY FANTASIZED ABOUT DOING?
HEY, HROAR -- FANCY SHARING A SADDLE? THERE'S ROOM FOR TWO ON STORMFLY.
I DON'T KNOW WHAT STINGS MORE, TOOTHLESS. THAT SHE SAID IT...
FEH.
...OR THAT SHE COULD BE RIGHT.

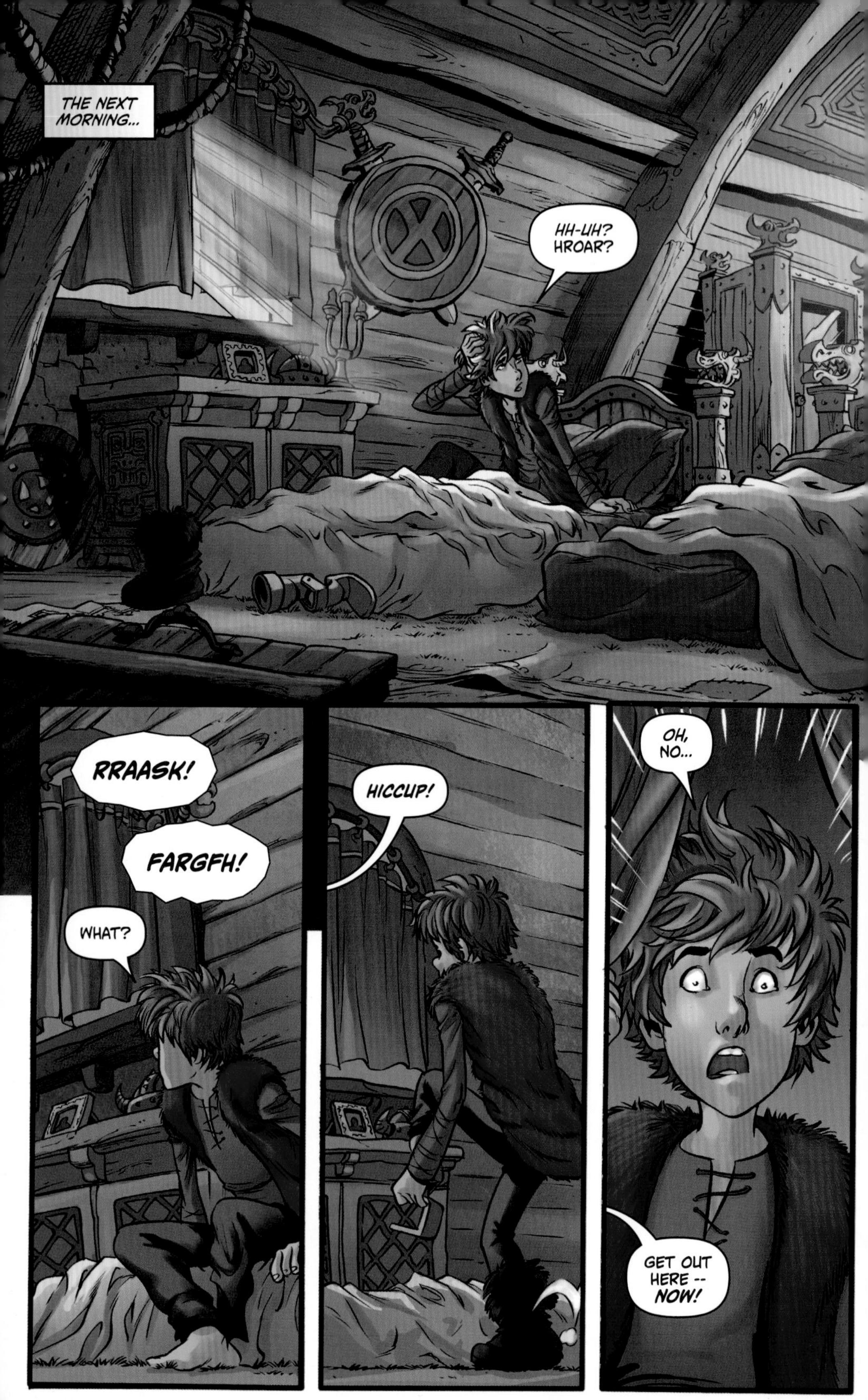
THE NEXT MORNING...
HH-UH? HROAR?
RRAASK!
FARGFH!
WHAT?
HICCUP!
OH, NO...
GET OUT HERE -- NOW!

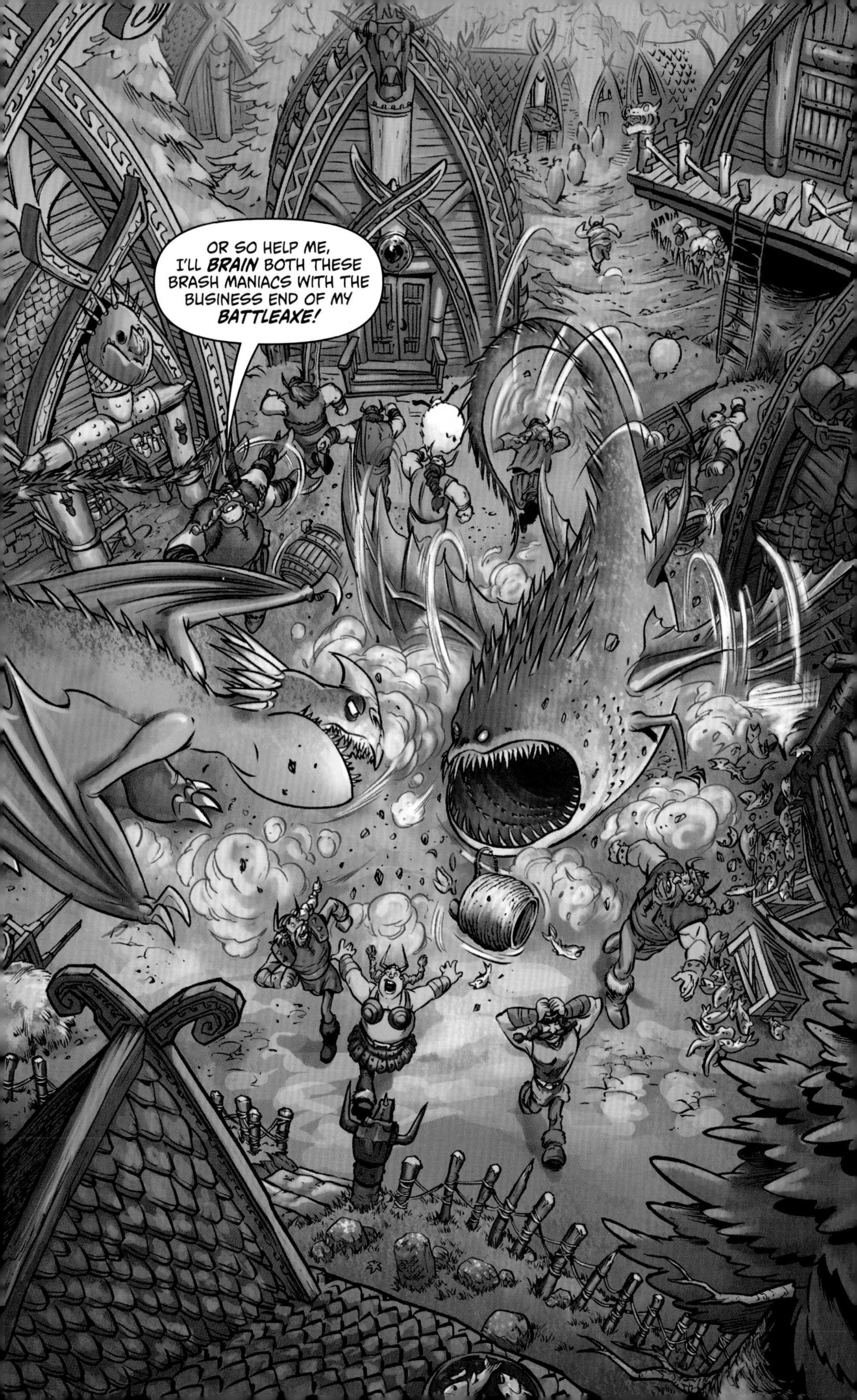
OR SO HELP ME, I'LL BRAIN BOTH THESE BRASH MANIACS WITH THE BUSINESS END OF MY BATTLEAXE!

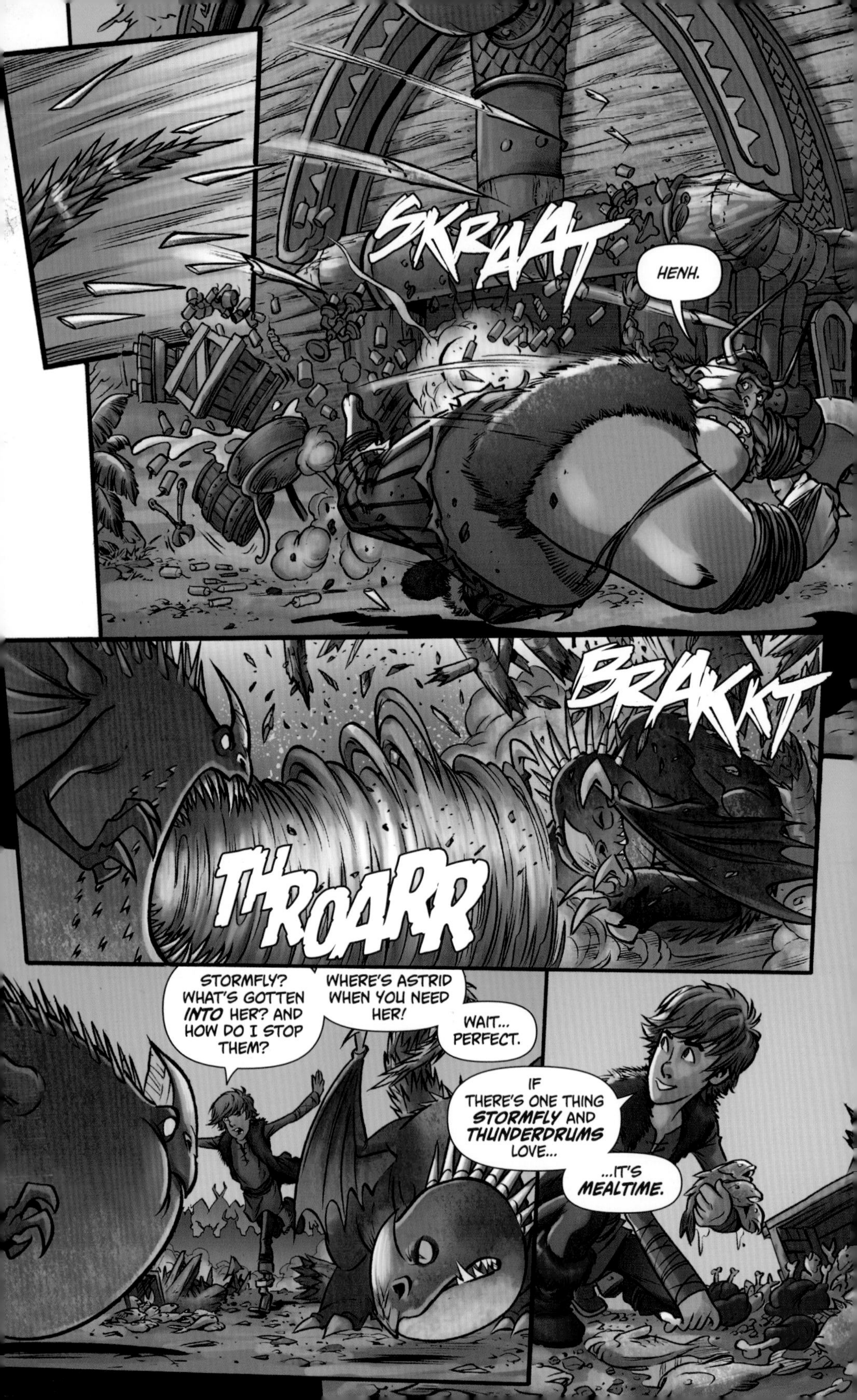
SKRAAAT
HENH.
BRAKKT
THROARR
STORMFLY? WHAT'S GOTTEN INTO HER? AND HOW DO I STOP THEM?
WHERE'S ASTRID WHEN YOU NEED HER!
WAIT... PERFECT.
IF THERE'S ONE THING STORMFLY AND THUNDERDRUMS LOVE...
...IT'S MEALTIME.

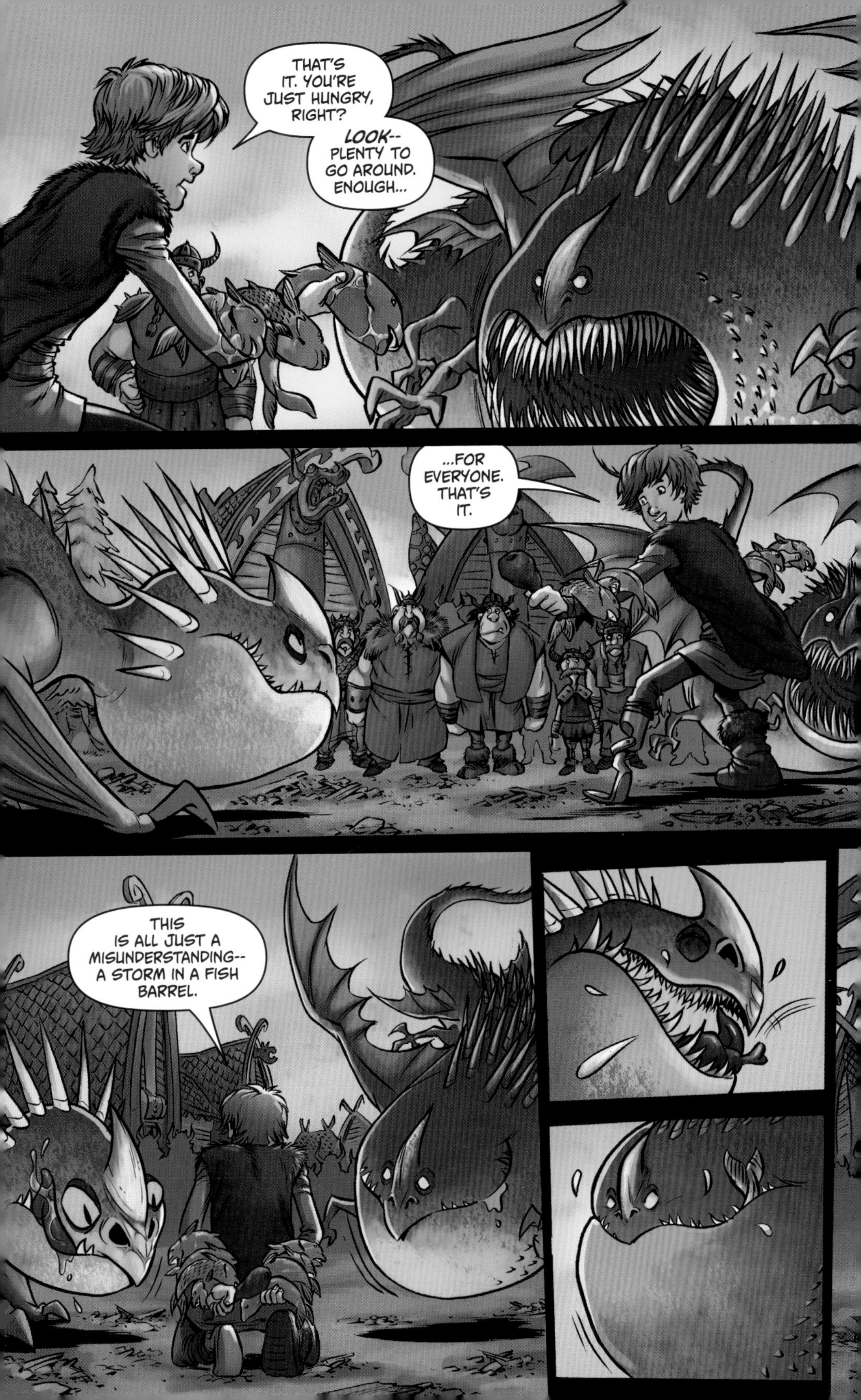
THAT'S IT. YOU'RE JUST HUNGRY, RIGHT?
LOOK-- PLENTY TO GO AROUND. ENOUGH...
...FOR EVERYONE. THAT'S IT.
THIS IS ALL JUST A MISUNDERSTANDING-- A STORM IN A FISH BARREL.

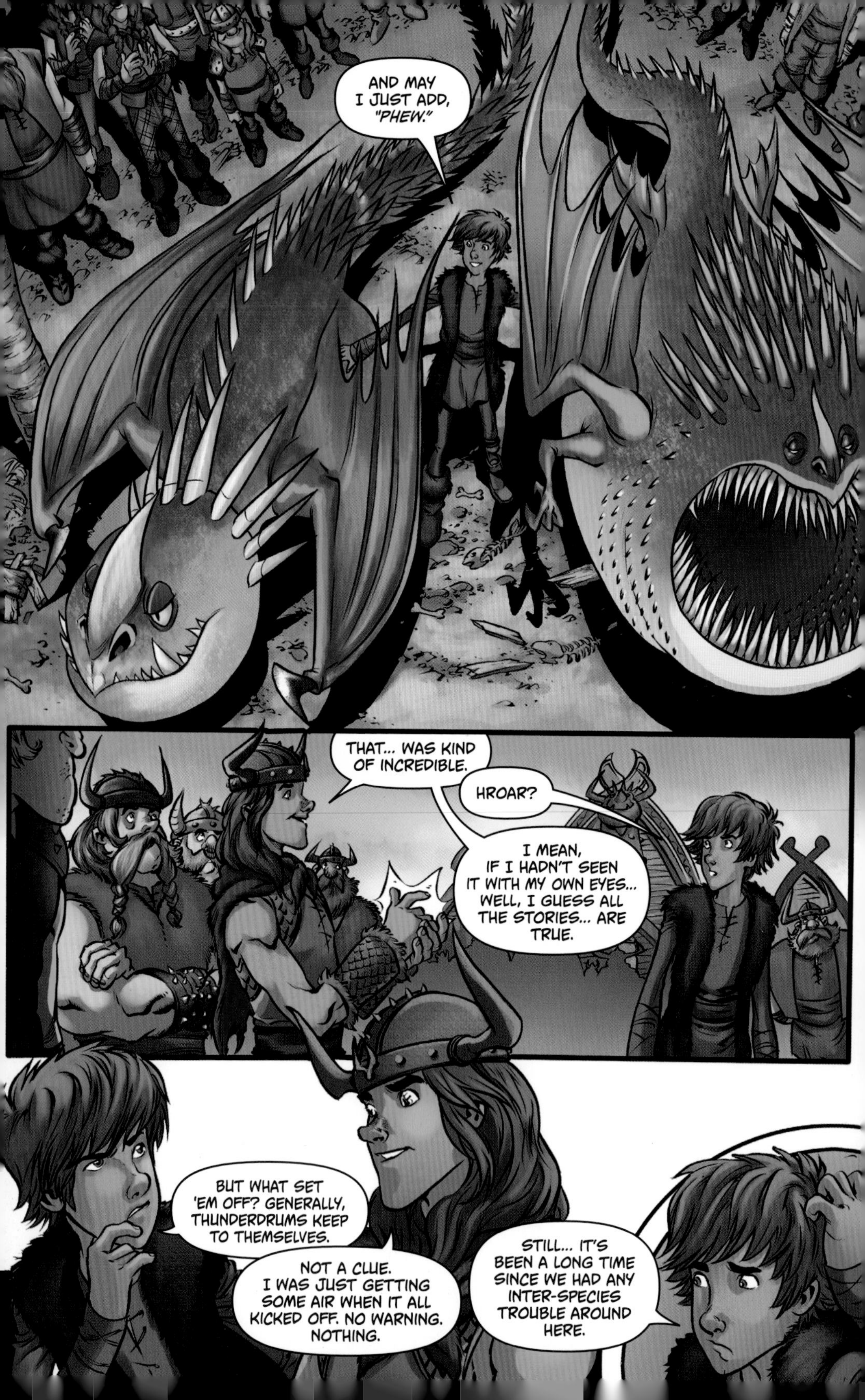
AND MAY I JUST ADD, "PHEW."
THAT... WAS KIND OF INCREDIBLE.
HROAR?
I MEAN, IF I HADN'T SEEN IT WITH MY OWN EYES... WELL, I GUESS ALL THE STORIES... ARE TRUE.
BUT WHAT SET 'EM OFF? GENERALLY, THUNDERDRUMS KEEP TO THEMSELVES.
NOT A CLUE. I WAS JUST GETTING SOME AIR WHEN IT ALL KICKED OFF. NO WARNING. NOTHING.
STILL... IT'S BEEN A LONG TIME SINCE WE HAD ANY INTER-SPECIES TROUBLE AROUND HERE.

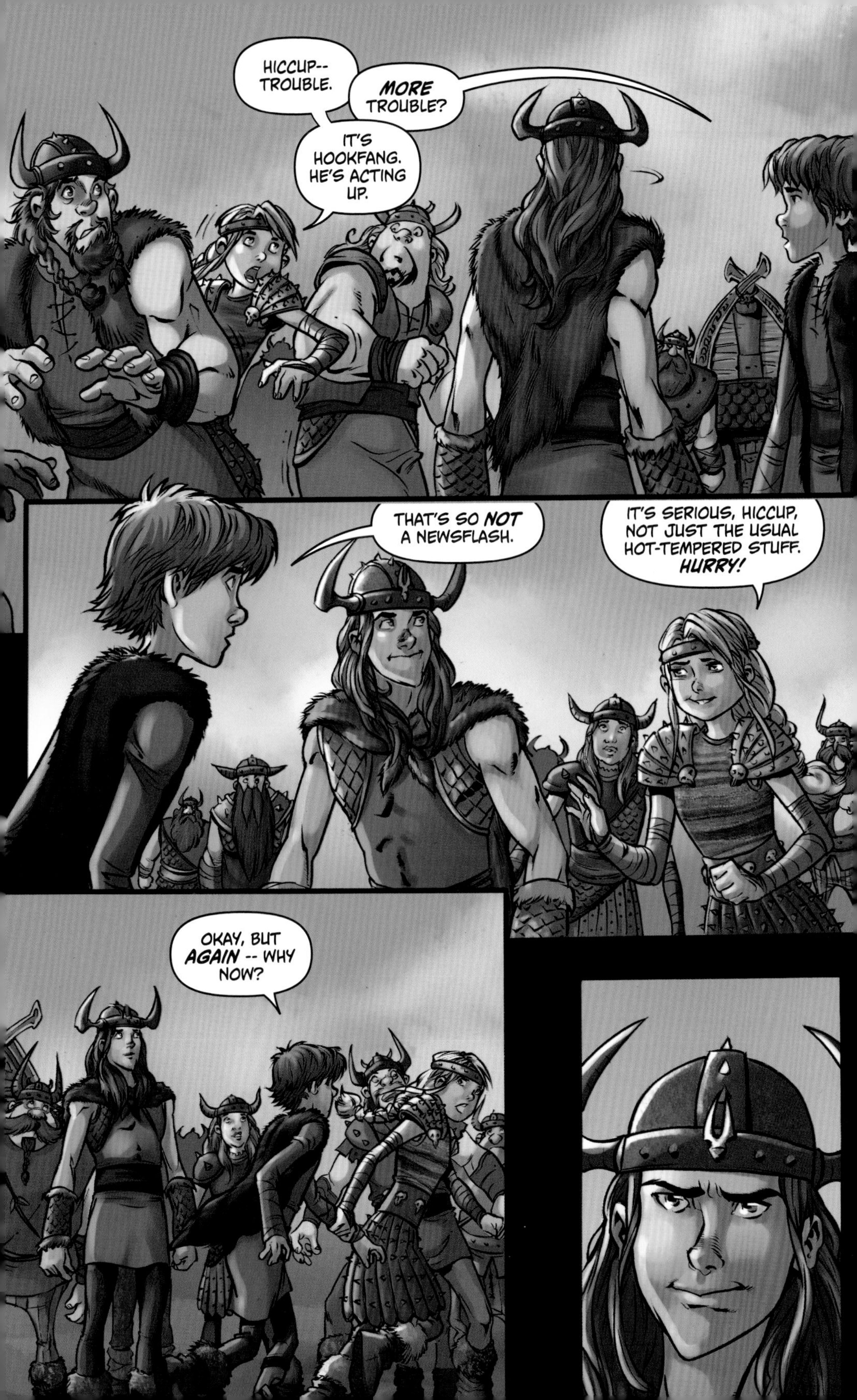
HICCUP-- TROUBLE.
MORE TROUBLE?
IT'S HOOKFANG. HE'S ACTING UP.
THAT'S SO NOT A NEWSFLASH.
IT'S SERIOUS, HICCUP, NOT JUST THE USUAL HOT-TEMPERED STUFF. HURRY!
OKAY, BUT AGAIN -- WHY NOW?

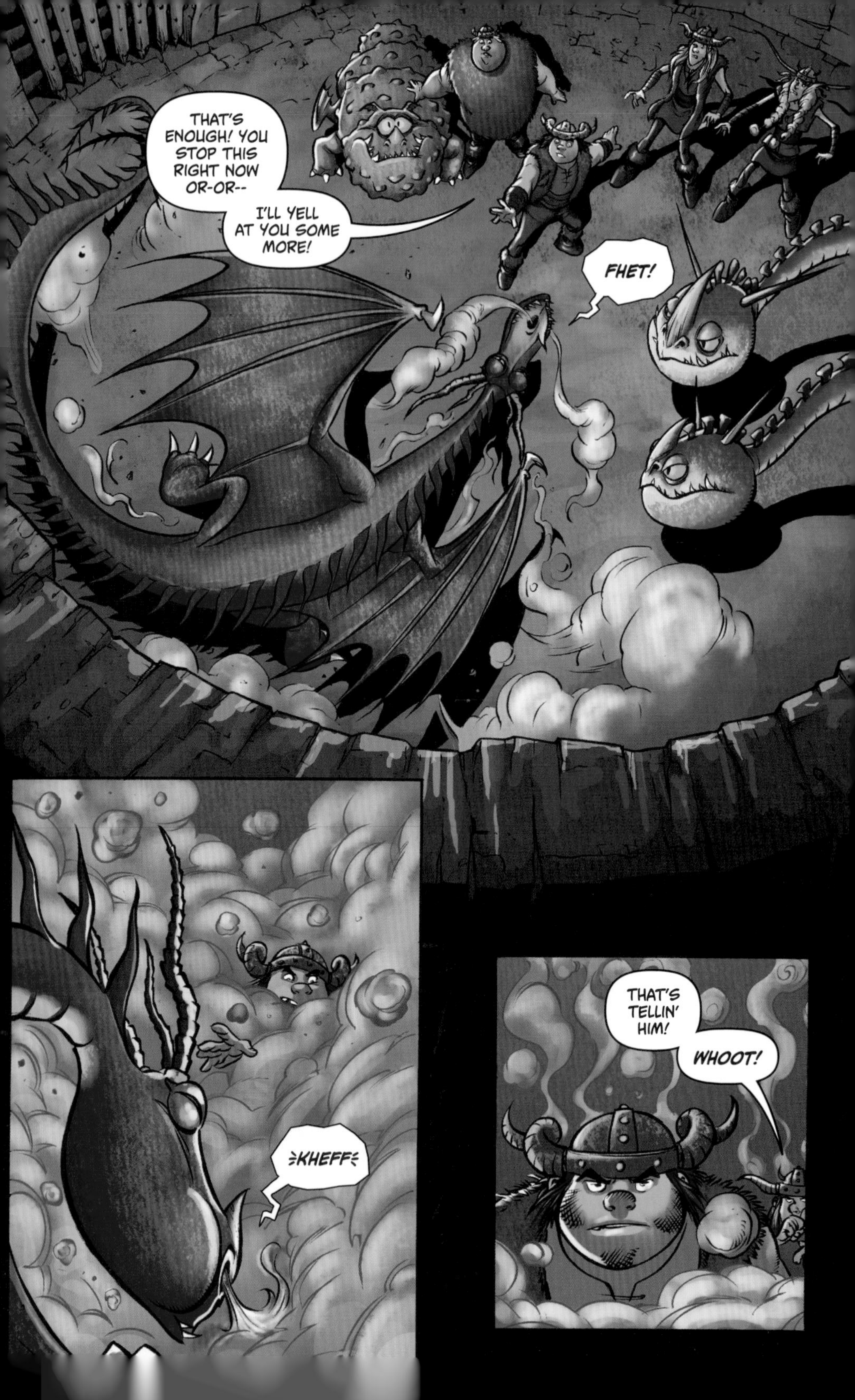
THAT'S ENOUGH! YOU STOP THIS RIGHT NOW OR-OR--
I'LL YELL AT YOU SOME MORE!
FHET!
KHEFF
THAT'S TELLIN' HIM!
WHOOT!

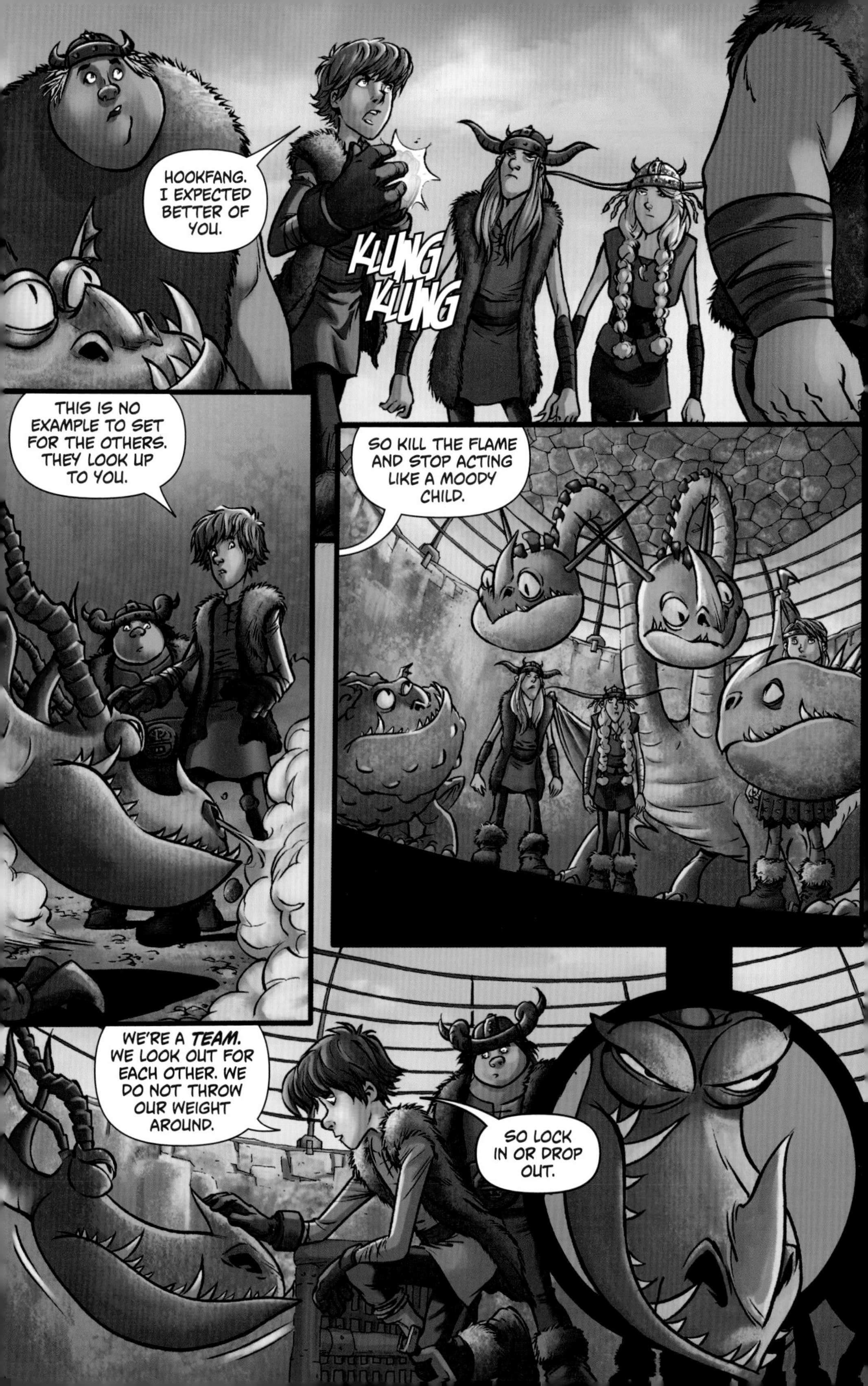
HOOKFANG. I EXPECTED BETTER OF YOU.
KLUNG KLUNG
THIS IS NO EXAMPLE TO SET FOR THE OTHERS. THEY LOOK UP TO YOU.
SO KILL THE FLAME AND STOP ACTING LIKE A MOODY CHILD.
WE'RE A *TEAM*. WE LOOK OUT FOR EACH OTHER. WE DO NOT THROW OUR WEIGHT AROUND.
SO LOCK IN OR DROP OUT.

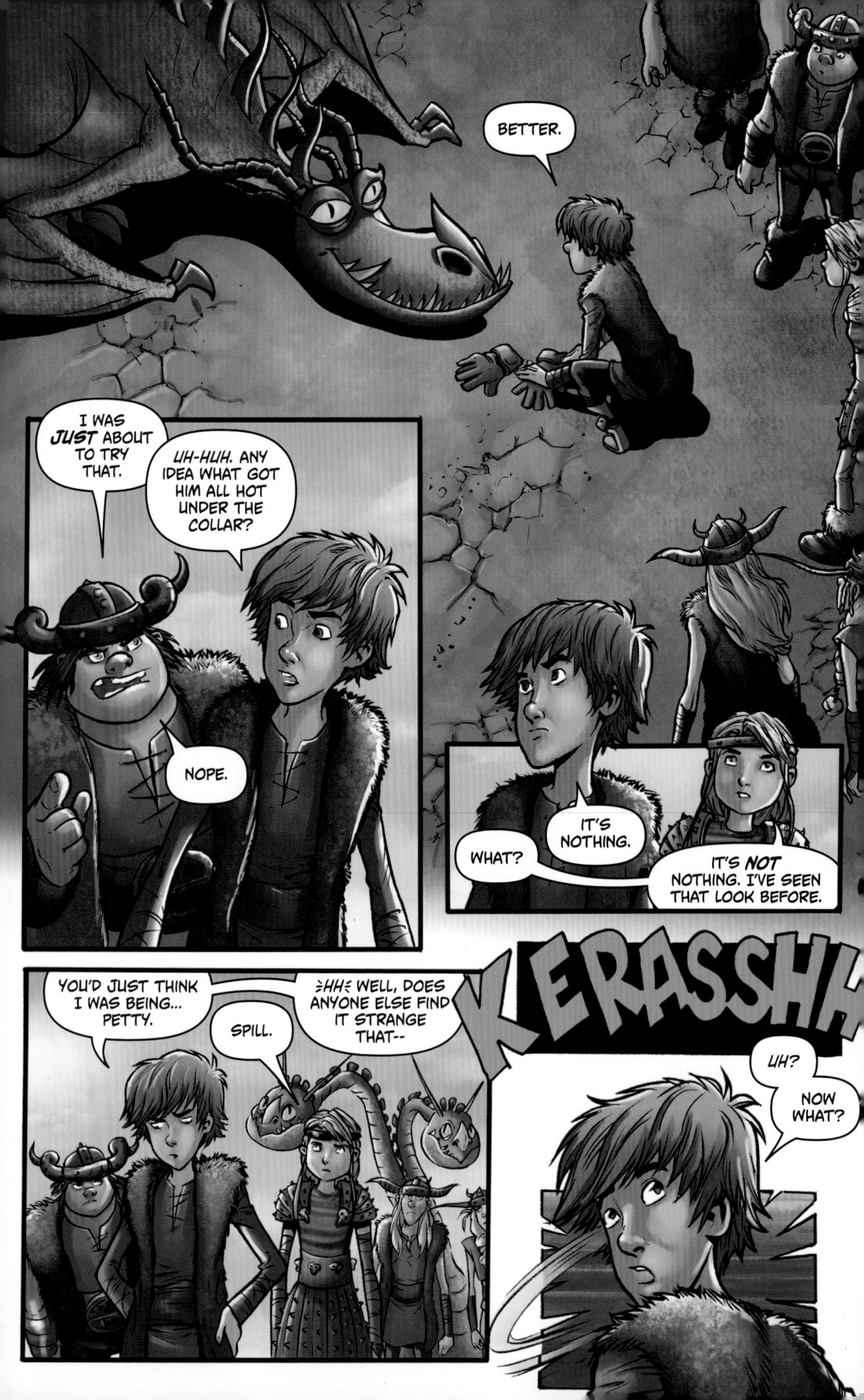
BETTER.
I WAS JUST ABOUT TO TRY THAT.
UH-HUH. ANY IDEA WHAT GOT HIM ALL HOT UNDER THE COLLAR?
NOPE.
IT'S NOTHING.
WHAT?
IT'S NOT NOTHING. I'VE SEEN THAT LOOK BEFORE.
YOU'D JUST THINK I WAS BEING... PETTY.
SPILL.
HH WELL, DOES ANYONE ELSE FIND IT STRANGE THAT--
KERASSHH
UH?
NOW WHAT?

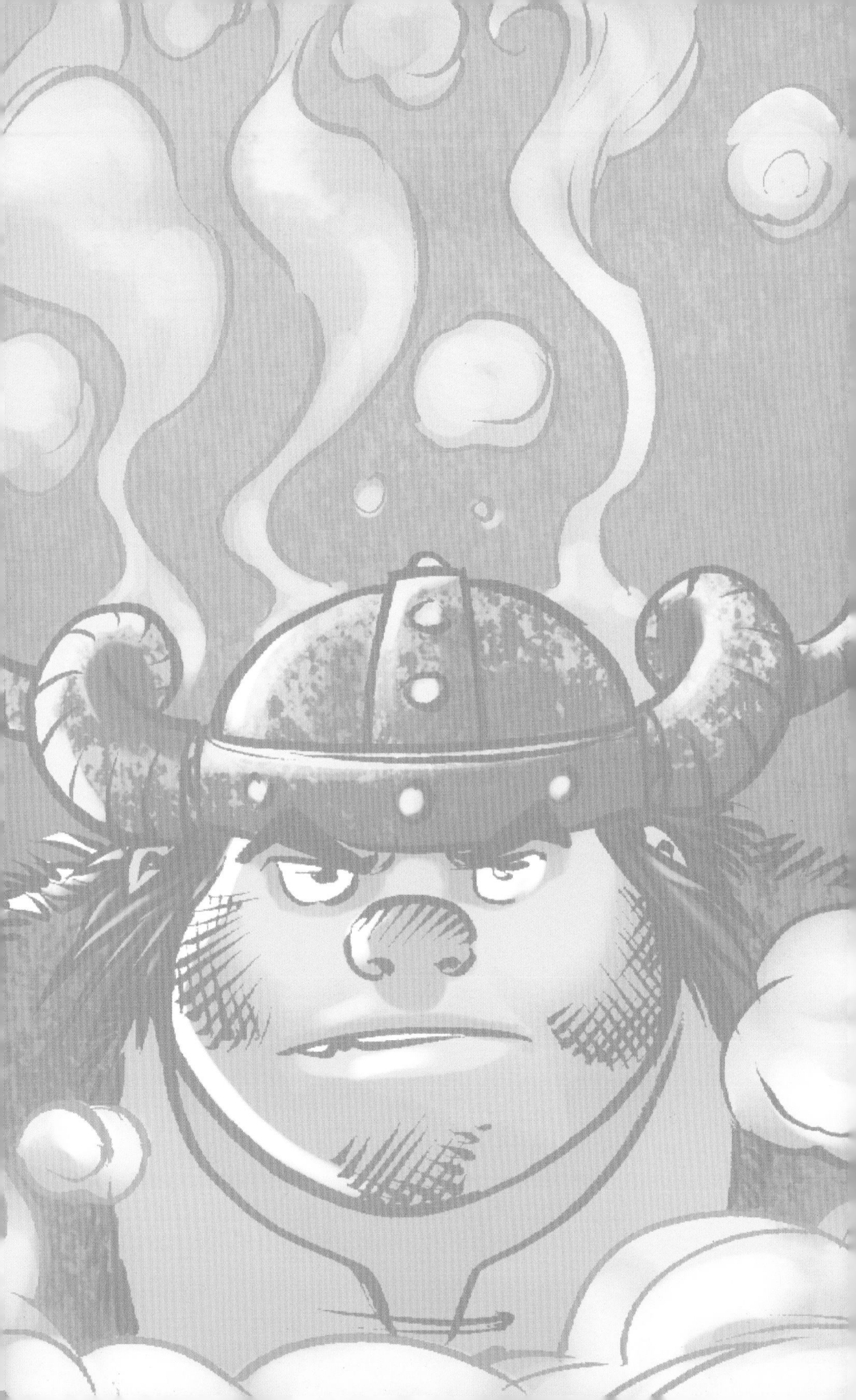

CHAPTER THREE

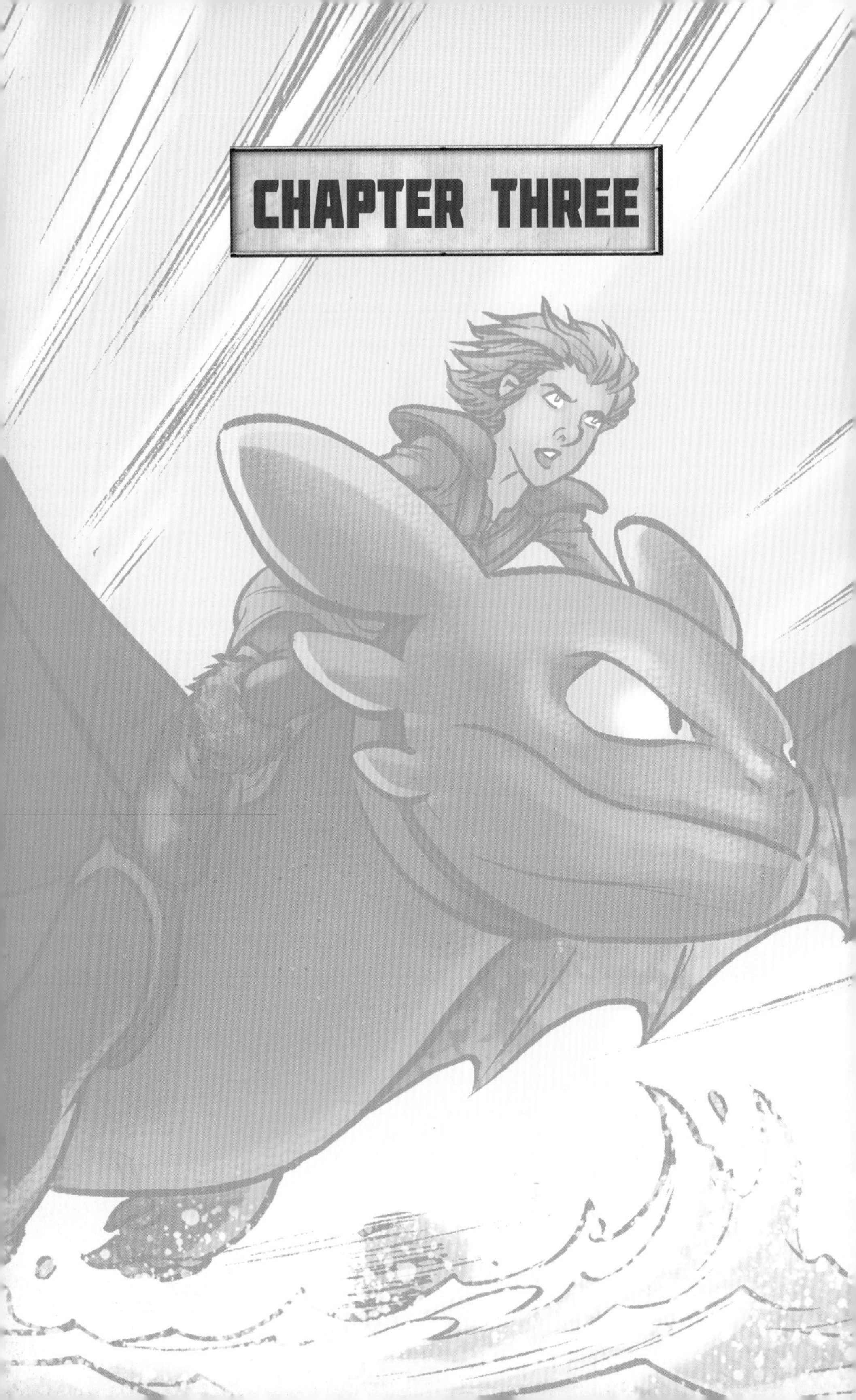

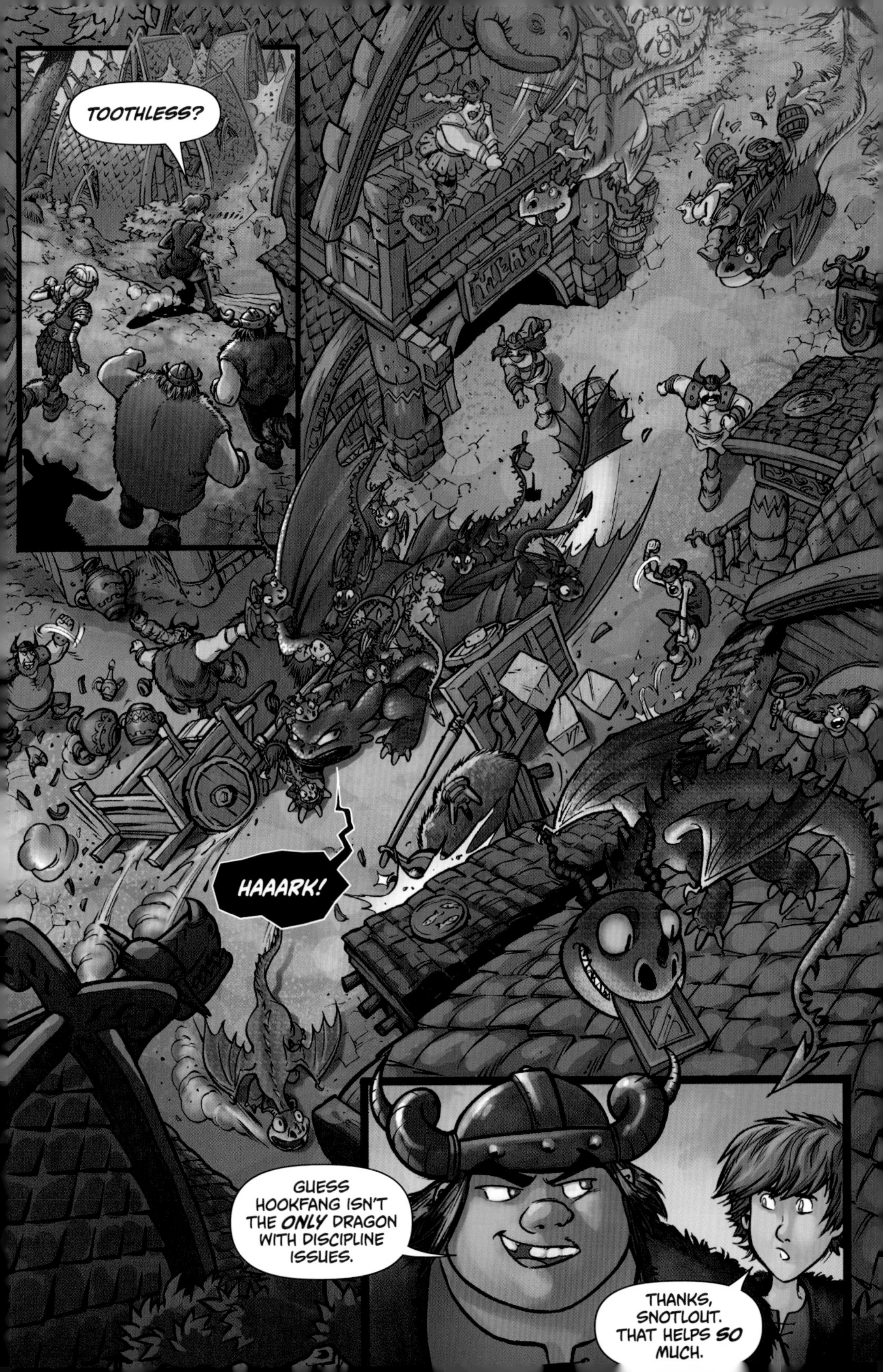
TOOTHLESS?
HAAARK!
GUESS HOOKFANG ISN'T THE ONLY DRAGON WITH DISCIPLINE ISSUES.
THANKS, SNOTLOUT. THAT HELPS SO MUCH.

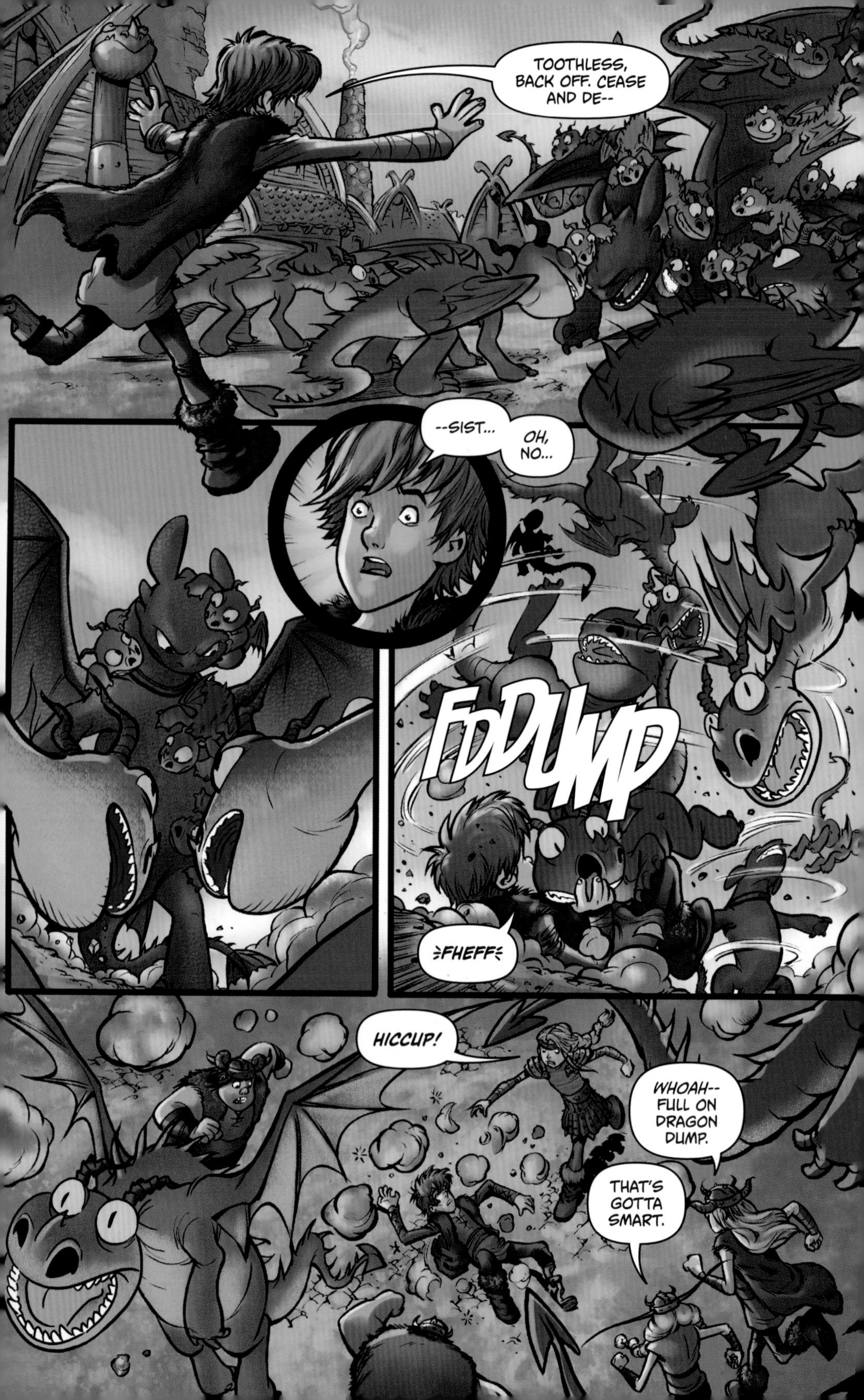
TOOTHLESS, BACK OFF. CEASE AND DE--
--SIST...
OH, NO...
FDDUMP
FHEFF
HICCUP!
WHOAH-- FULL ON DRAGON DUMP.
THAT'S GOTTA SMART.

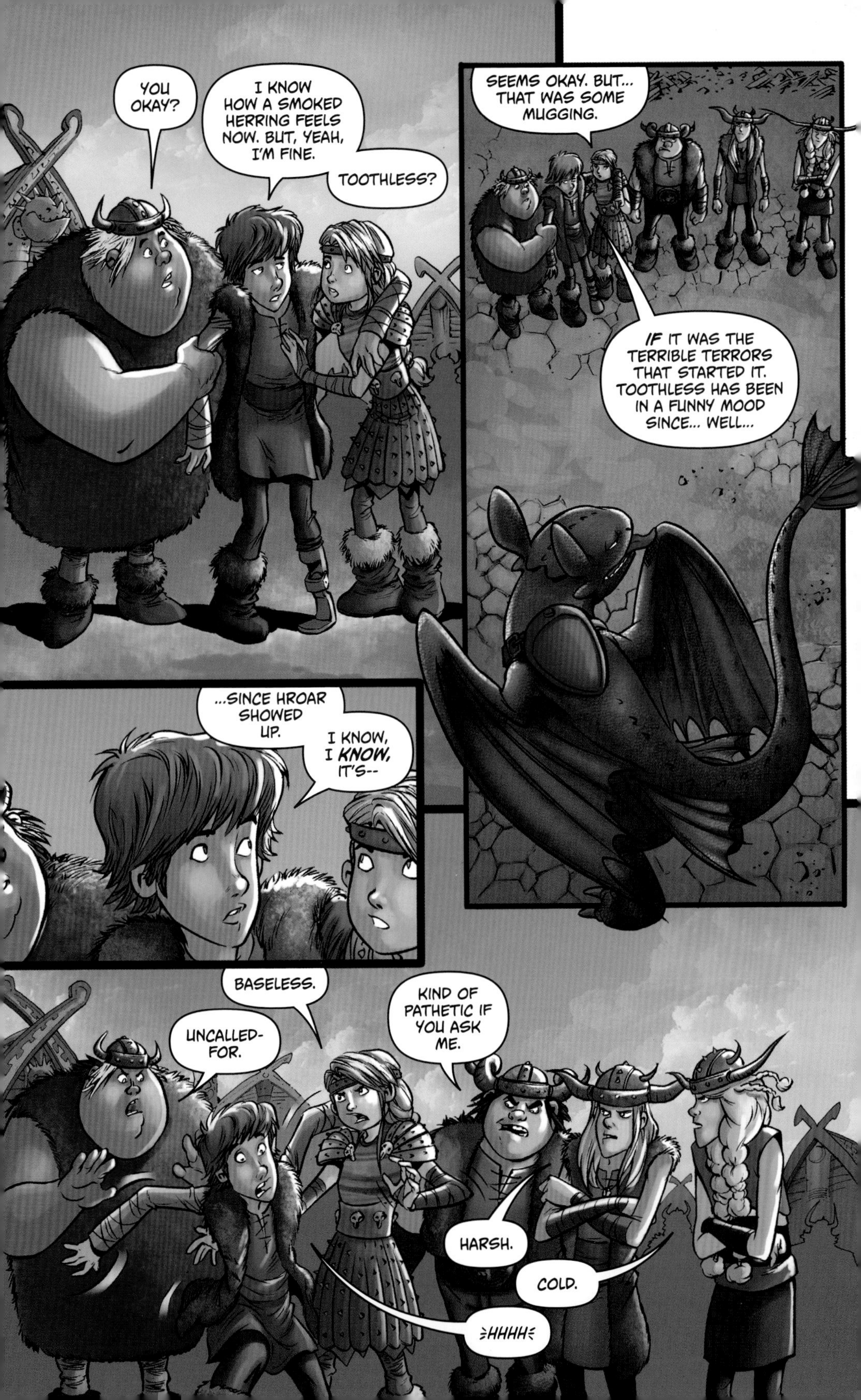
YOU OKAY?
I KNOW HOW A SMOKED HERRING FEELS NOW. BUT, YEAH, I'M FINE.
TOOTHLESS?
SEEMS OKAY. BUT... THAT WAS SOME MUGGING.
IF IT WAS THE TERRIBLE TERRORS THAT STARTED IT. TOOTHLESS HAS BEEN IN A FUNNY MOOD SINCE... WELL...
...SINCE HROAR SHOWED UP.
I KNOW, I *KNOW,* IT'S--
BASELESS.
UNCALLED-FOR.
KIND OF PATHETIC IF YOU ASK ME.
HARSH.
COLD.
HHHH

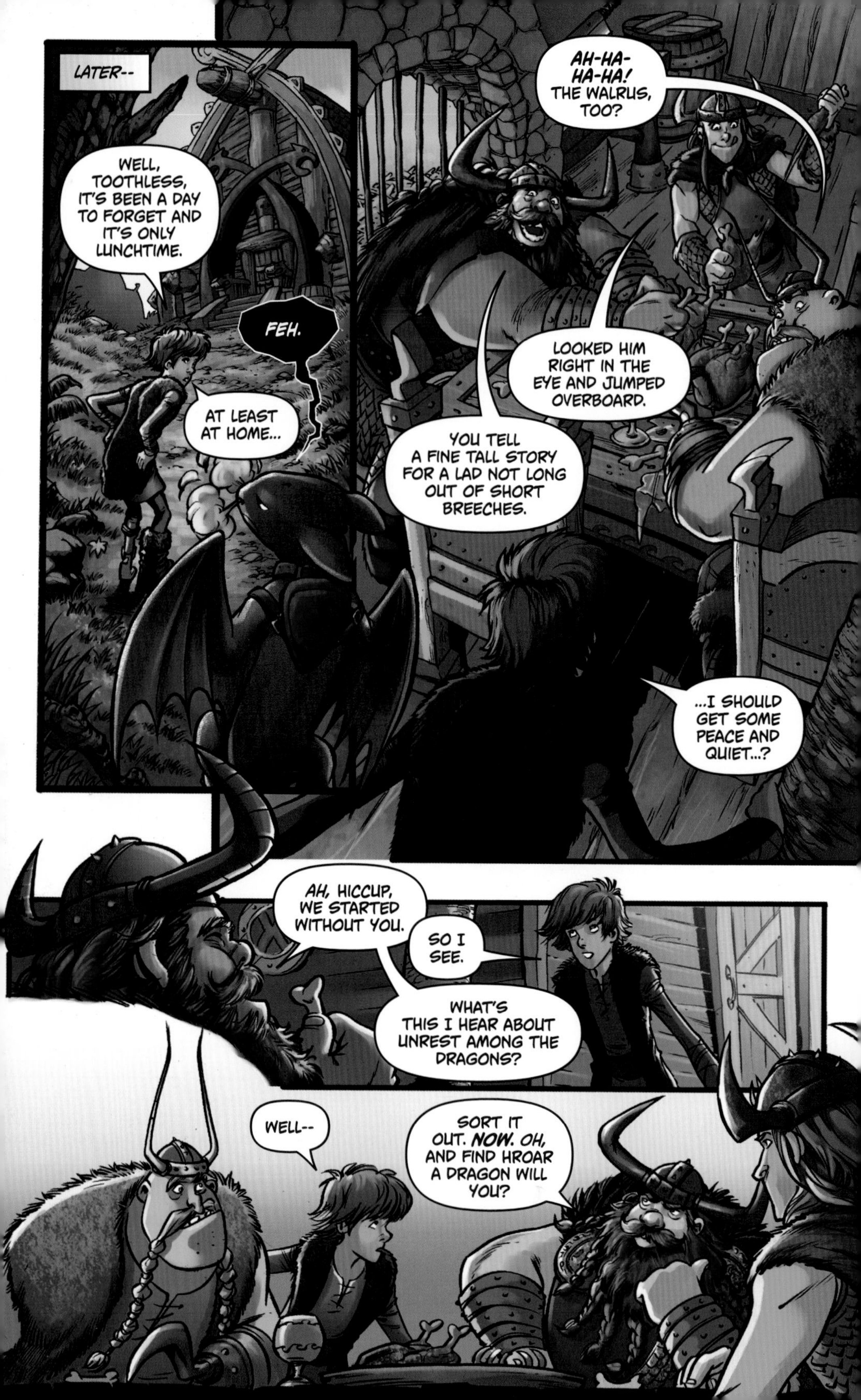
LATER--
WELL, TOOTHLESS, IT'S BEEN A DAY TO FORGET AND IT'S ONLY LUNCHTIME.
FEH.
AT LEAST AT HOME...
AH-HA-HA-HA! THE WALRUS, TOO?
LOOKED HIM RIGHT IN THE EYE AND JUMPED OVERBOARD.
YOU TELL A FINE TALL STORY FOR A LAD NOT LONG OUT OF SHORT BREECHES.
...I SHOULD GET SOME PEACE AND QUIET...?
AH, HICCUP, WE STARTED WITHOUT YOU.
SO I SEE.
WHAT'S THIS I HEAR ABOUT UNREST AMONG THE DRAGONS?
WELL--
SORT IT OUT. NOW. OH, AND FIND HROAR A DRAGON WILL YOU?

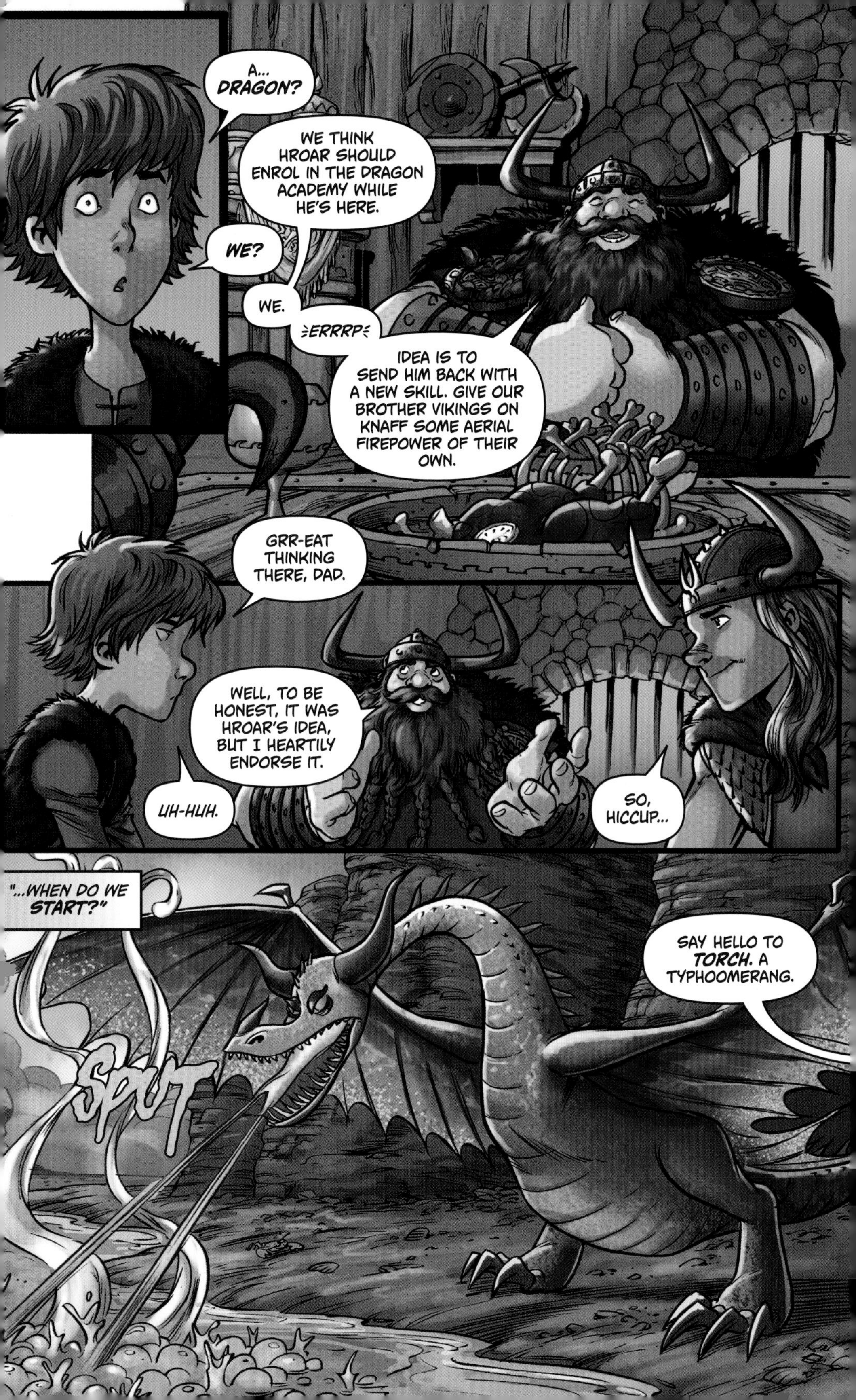
A... DRAGON?
WE THINK HROAR SHOULD ENROL IN THE DRAGON ACADEMY WHILE HE'S HERE.
WE?
WE.
ERRRP
IDEA IS TO SEND HIM BACK WITH A NEW SKILL. GIVE OUR BROTHER VIKINGS ON KNAFF SOME AERIAL FIREPOWER OF THEIR OWN.
GRR-EAT THINKING THERE, DAD.
WELL, TO BE HONEST, IT WAS HROAR'S IDEA, BUT I HEARTILY ENDORSE IT.
UH-HUH.
SO, HICCUP...
"...WHEN DO WE START?"
SAY HELLO TO TORCH. A TYPHOOMERANG.
SPUT

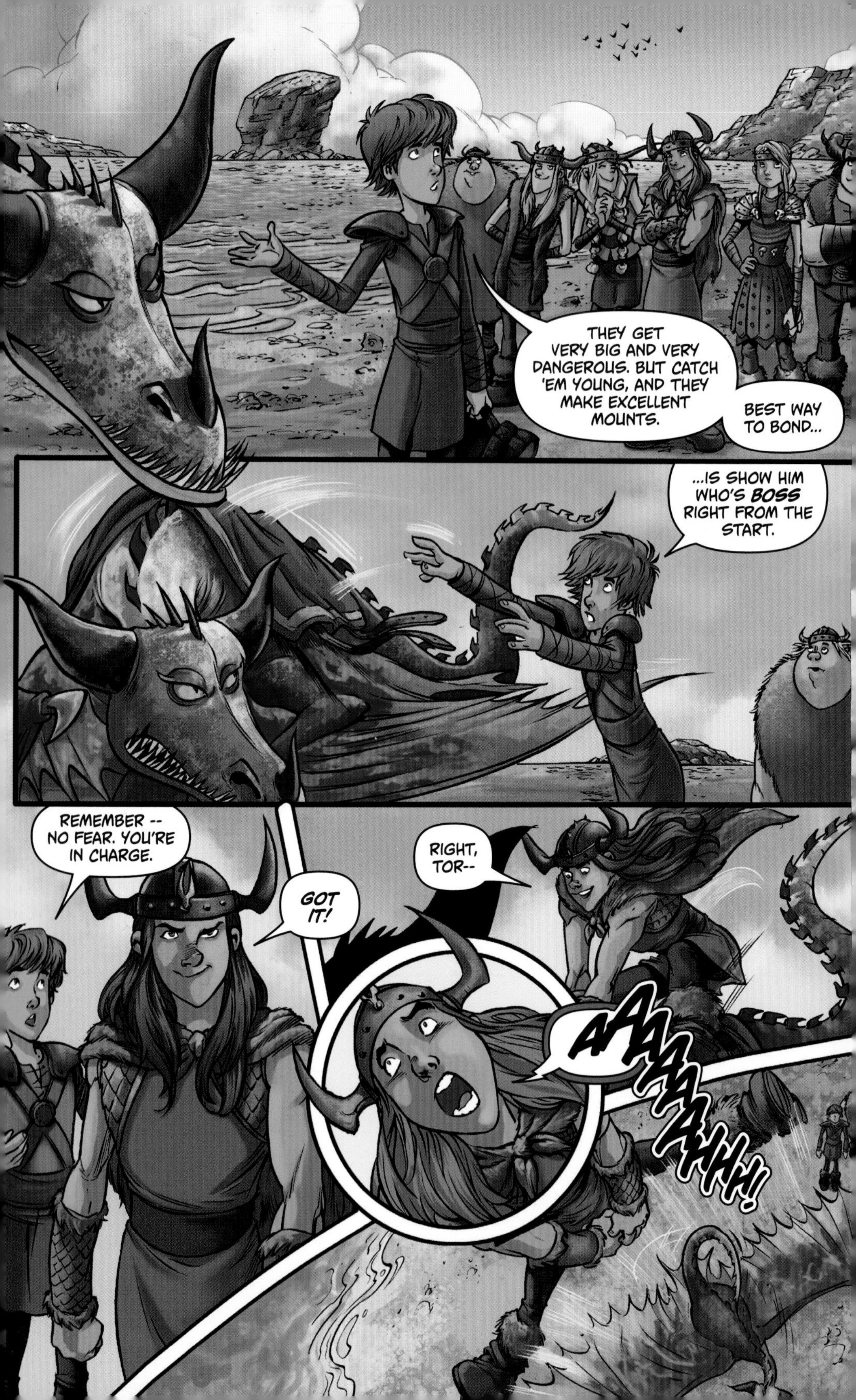
THEY GET VERY BIG AND VERY DANGEROUS. BUT CATCH 'EM YOUNG, AND THEY MAKE EXCELLENT MOUNTS.
BEST WAY TO BOND...
...IS SHOW HIM WHO'S **BOSS** RIGHT FROM THE START.
REMEMBER -- NO FEAR. YOU'RE IN CHARGE.
GOT IT!
RIGHT, TOR--
AAAAAAAHHH!!

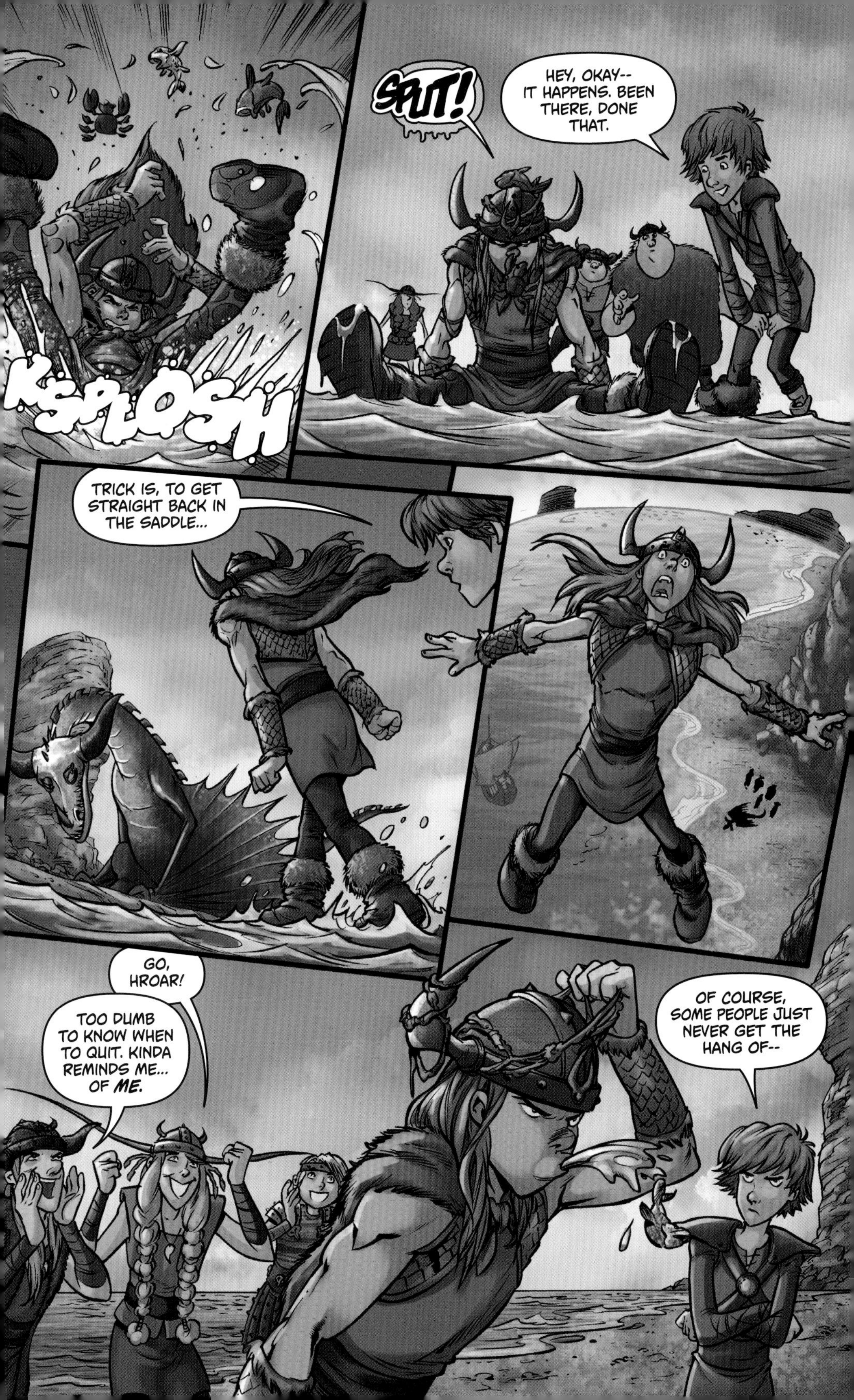
KSPLOSH
SPLIT!
HEY, OKAY-- IT HAPPENS. BEEN THERE, DONE THAT.
TRICK IS, TO GET STRAIGHT BACK IN THE SADDLE...
GO, HROAR!
TOO DUMB TO KNOW WHEN TO QUIT. KINDA REMINDS ME... OF ME.
OF COURSE, SOME PEOPLE JUST NEVER GET THE HANG OF--

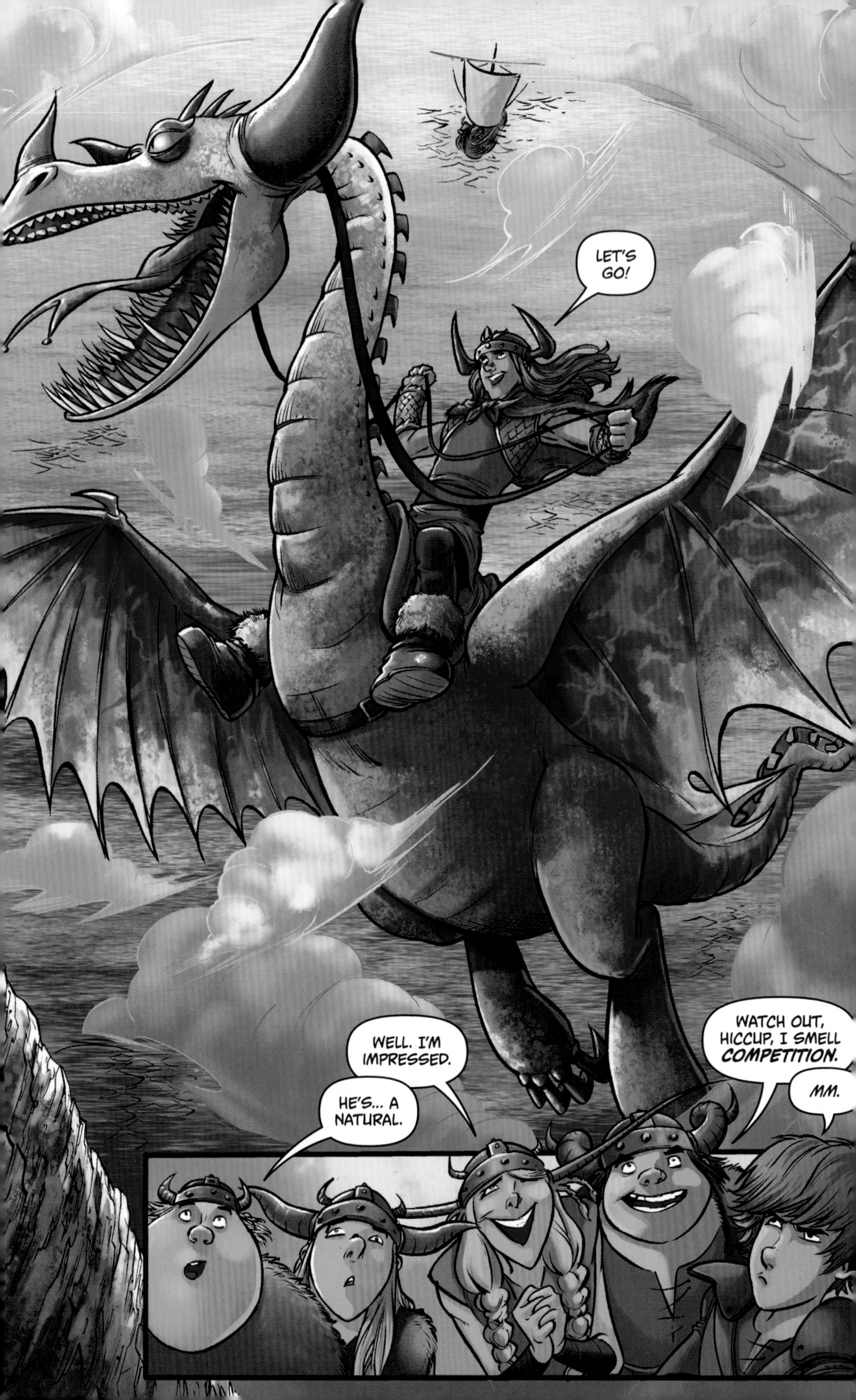
LET'S GO!
WELL. I'M IMPRESSED.
HE'S... A NATURAL.
WATCH OUT, HICCUP, I SMELL COMPETITION.
MM.

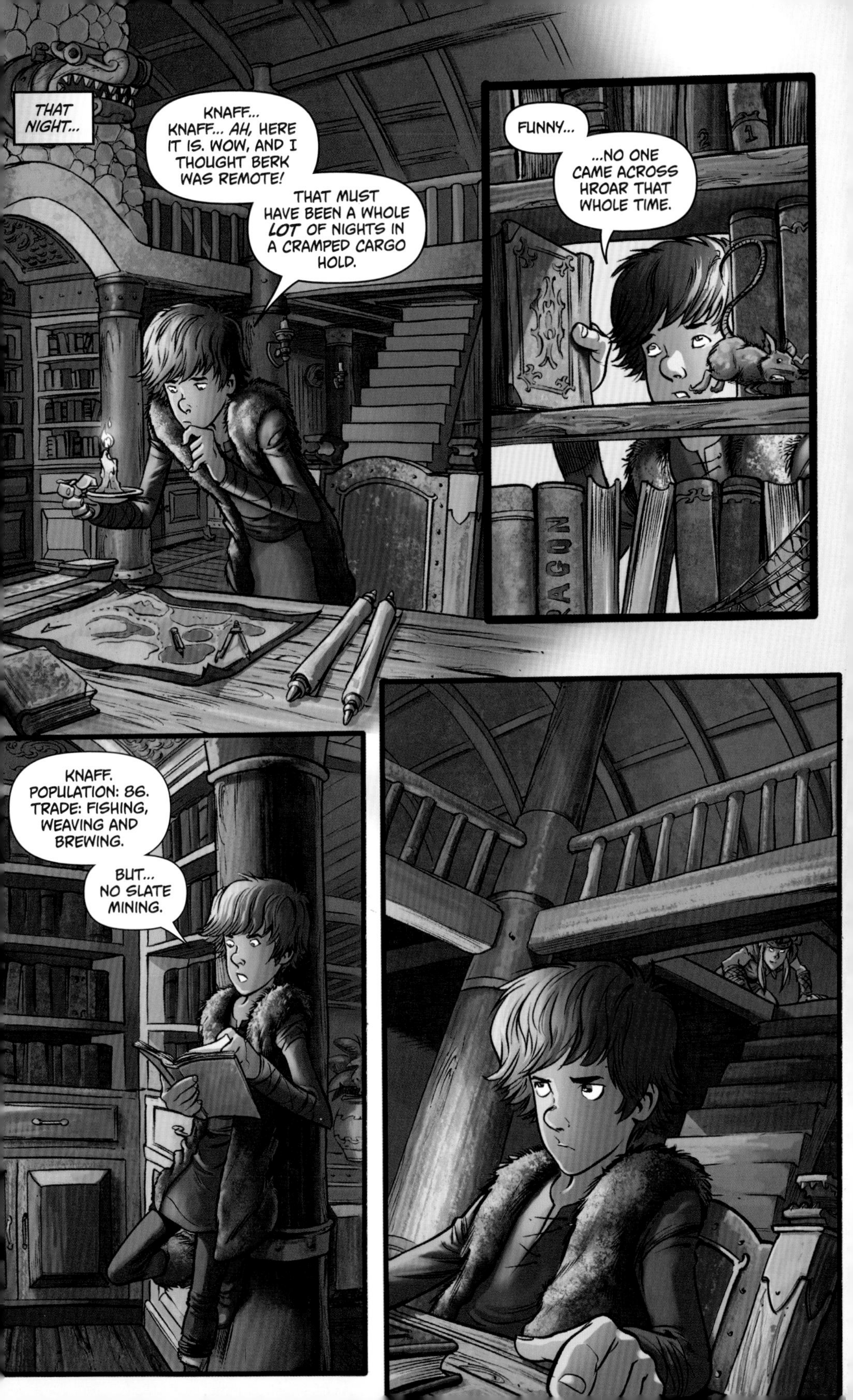

THAT NIGHT...
KNAFF... KNAFF... AH, HERE IT IS. WOW, AND I THOUGHT BERK WAS REMOTE!
THAT MUST HAVE BEEN A WHOLE LOT OF NIGHTS IN A CRAMPED CARGO HOLD.
FUNNY...
...NO ONE CAME ACROSS HROAR THAT WHOLE TIME.
KNAFF. POPULATION: 86. TRADE: FISHING, WEAVING AND BREWING.
BUT... NO SLATE MINING.

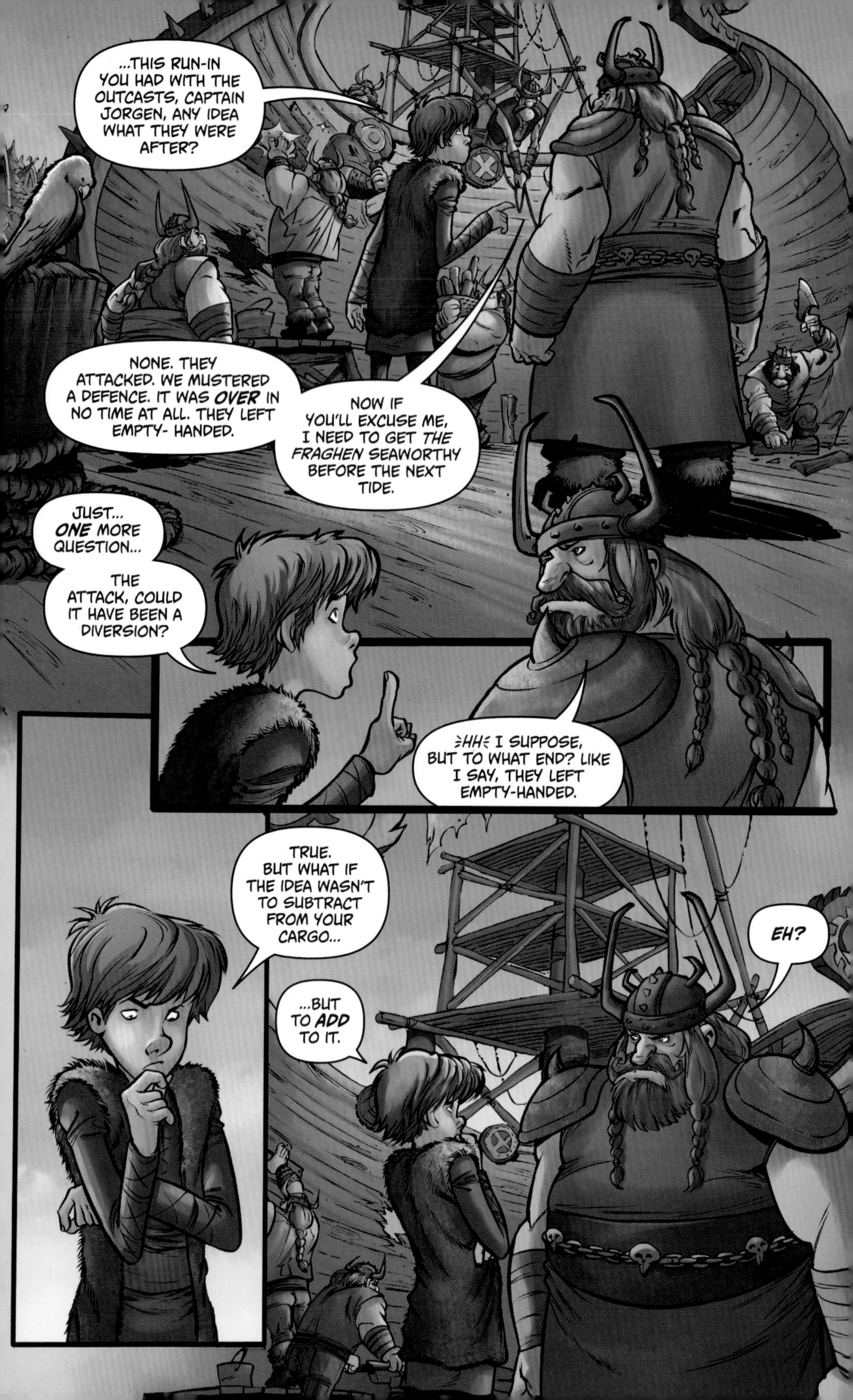
...THIS RUN-IN YOU HAD WITH THE OUTCASTS, CAPTAIN JORGEN, ANY IDEA WHAT THEY WERE AFTER?
NONE. THEY ATTACKED. WE MUSTERED A DEFENCE. IT WAS *OVER* IN NO TIME AT ALL. THEY LEFT EMPTY- HANDED.
NOW IF YOU'LL EXCUSE ME, I NEED TO GET *THE FRAGHEN* SEAWORTHY BEFORE THE NEXT TIDE.
JUST... *ONE* MORE QUESTION...
THE ATTACK, COULD IT HAVE BEEN A DIVERSION?
HH I SUPPOSE, BUT TO WHAT END? LIKE I SAY, THEY LEFT EMPTY-HANDED.
TRUE. BUT WHAT IF THE IDEA WASN'T TO SUBTRACT FROM YOUR CARGO...
...BUT TO *ADD* TO IT.
EH?

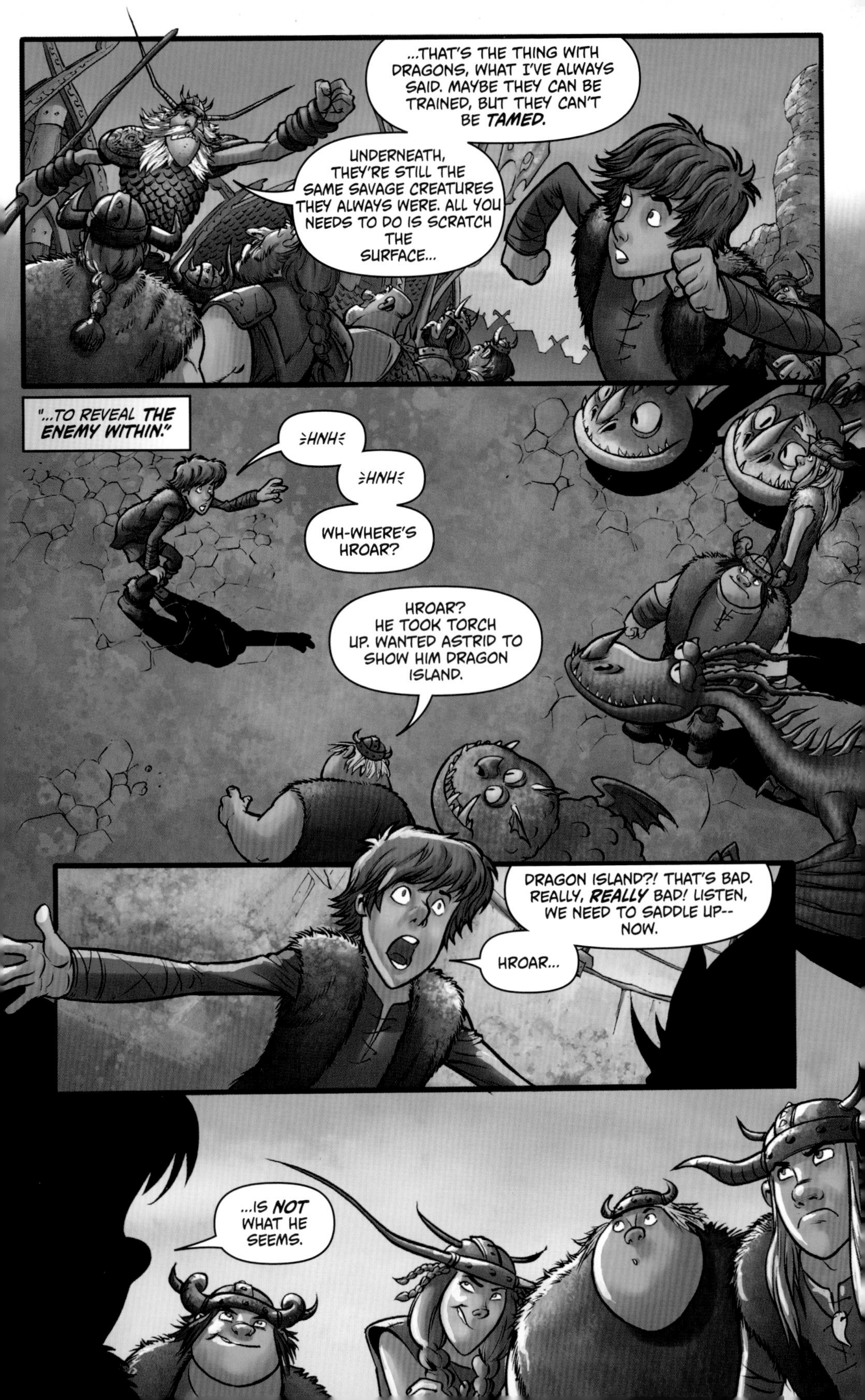
...THAT'S THE THING WITH DRAGONS, WHAT I'VE ALWAYS SAID. MAYBE THEY CAN BE TRAINED, BUT THEY CAN'T BE TAMED.
UNDERNEATH, THEY'RE STILL THE SAME SAVAGE CREATURES THEY ALWAYS WERE. ALL YOU NEEDS TO DO IS SCRATCH THE SURFACE...
"...TO REVEAL THE ENEMY WITHIN."
HNH
HNH
WH-WHERE'S HROAR?
HROAR? HE TOOK TORCH UP. WANTED ASTRID TO SHOW HIM DRAGON ISLAND.
DRAGON ISLAND?! THAT'S BAD. REALLY, REALLY BAD! LISTEN, WE NEED TO SADDLE UP-- NOW.
HROAR...
...IS NOT WHAT HE SEEMS.

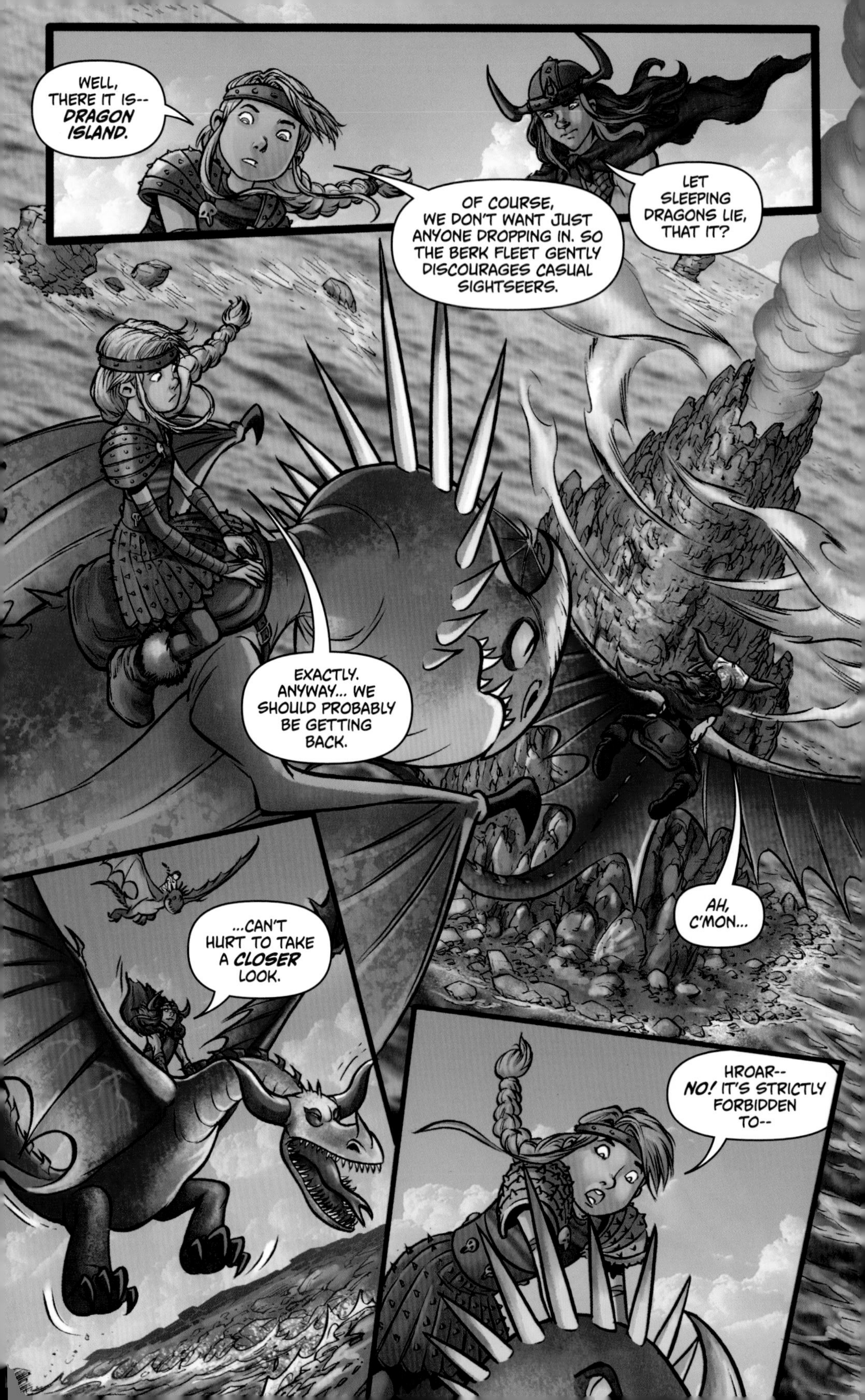
WELL, THERE IT IS-- DRAGON ISLAND.
OF COURSE, WE DON'T WANT JUST ANYONE DROPPING IN. SO THE BERK FLEET GENTLY DISCOURAGES CASUAL SIGHTSEERS.
LET SLEEPING DRAGONS LIE, THAT IT?
EXACTLY. ANYWAY... WE SHOULD PROBABLY BE GETTING BACK.
AH, C'MON...
...CAN'T HURT TO TAKE A CLOSER LOOK.
HROAR-- NO! IT'S STRICTLY FORBIDDEN TO--

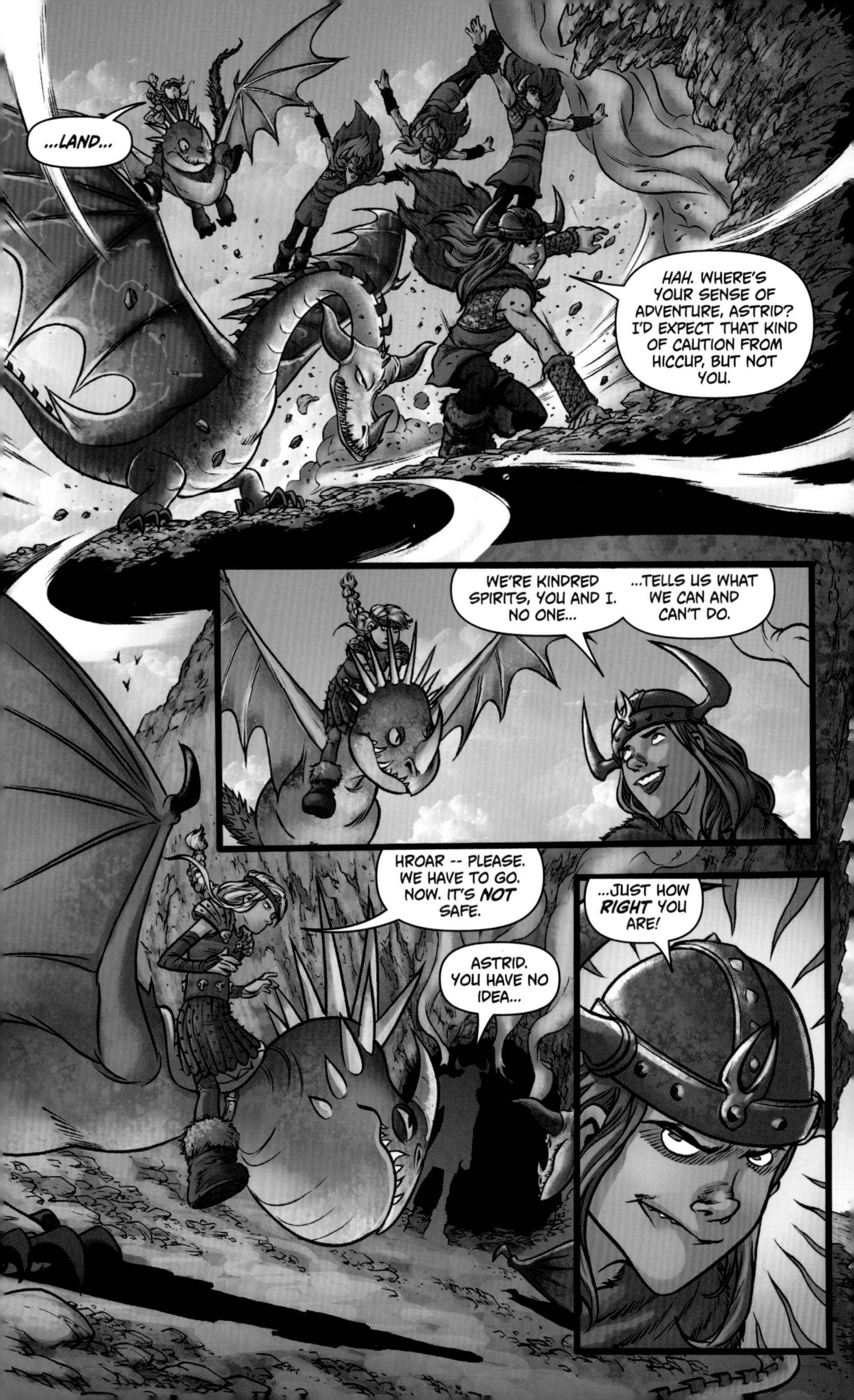
...LAND...
HAH. WHERE'S YOUR SENSE OF ADVENTURE, ASTRID? I'D EXPECT THAT KIND OF CAUTION FROM HICCUP, BUT NOT YOU.
WE'RE KINDRED SPIRITS, YOU AND I. NO ONE...
...TELLS US WHAT WE CAN AND CAN'T DO.
HROAR -- PLEASE. WE HAVE TO GO. NOW. IT'S *NOT* SAFE.
ASTRID. YOU HAVE NO IDEA...
...JUST HOW *RIGHT* YOU ARE!

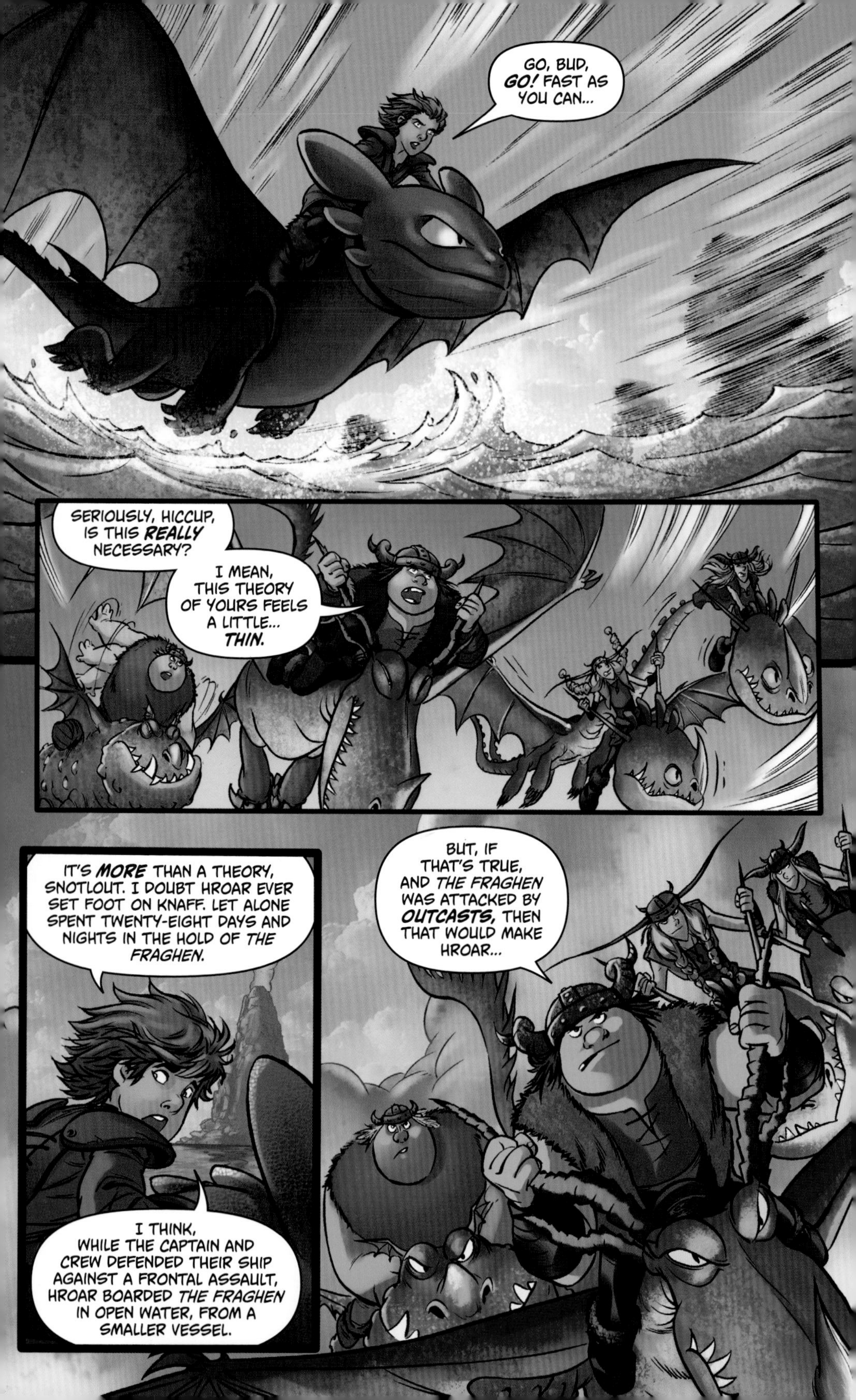
GO, BUD, GO! FAST AS YOU CAN...
SERIOUSLY, HICCUP, IS THIS REALLY NECESSARY?
I MEAN, THIS THEORY OF YOURS FEELS A LITTLE... THIN.
IT'S MORE THAN A THEORY, SNOTLOUT. I DOUBT HROAR EVER SET FOOT ON KNAFF. LET ALONE SPENT TWENTY-EIGHT DAYS AND NIGHTS IN THE HOLD OF THE FRAGHEN.
I THINK, WHILE THE CAPTAIN AND CREW DEFENDED THEIR SHIP AGAINST A FRONTAL ASSAULT, HROAR BOARDED THE FRAGHEN IN OPEN WATER, FROM A SMALLER VESSEL.
BUT, IF THAT'S TRUE, AND THE FRAGHEN WAS ATTACKED BY OUTCASTS, THEN THAT WOULD MAKE HROAR...

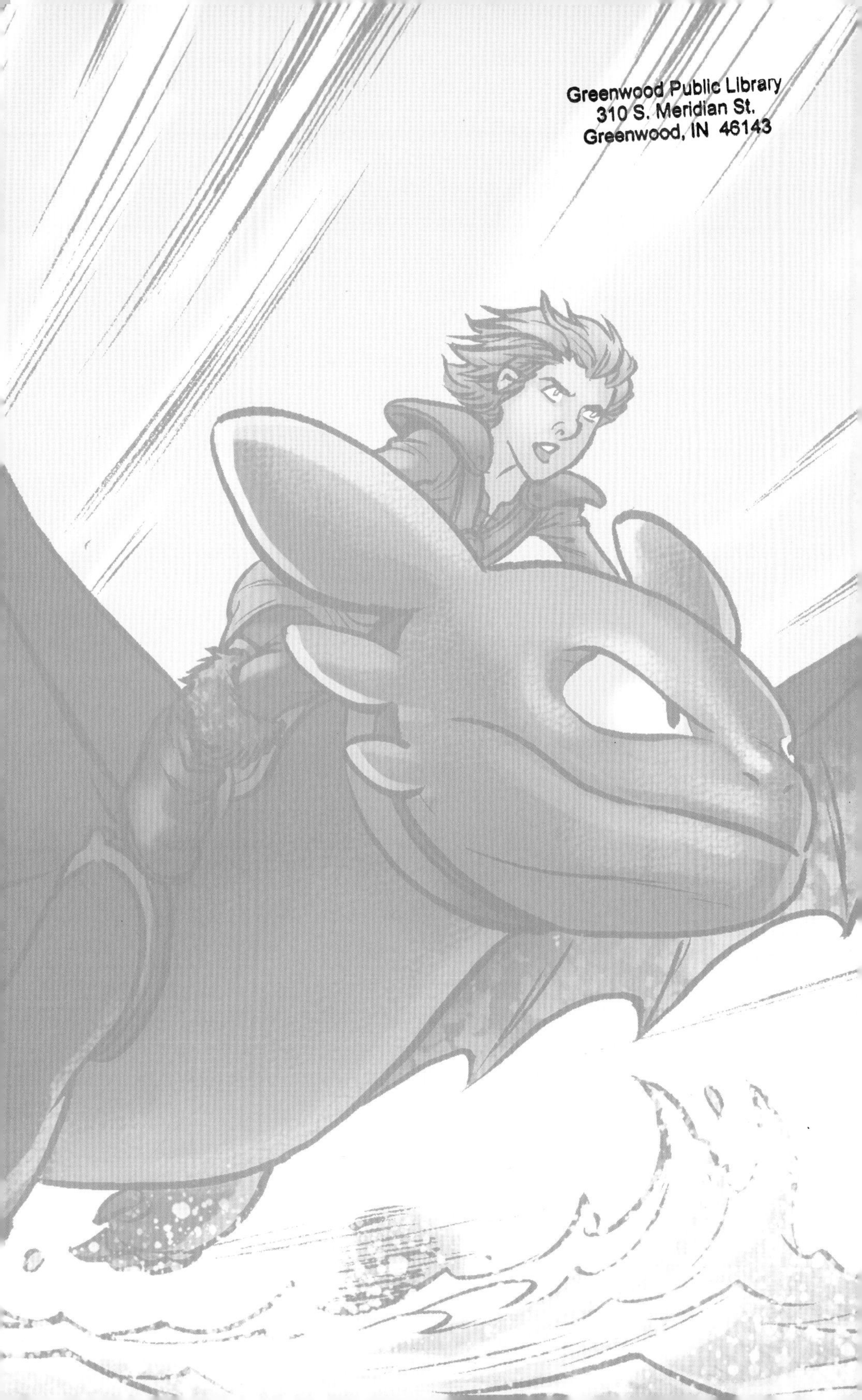

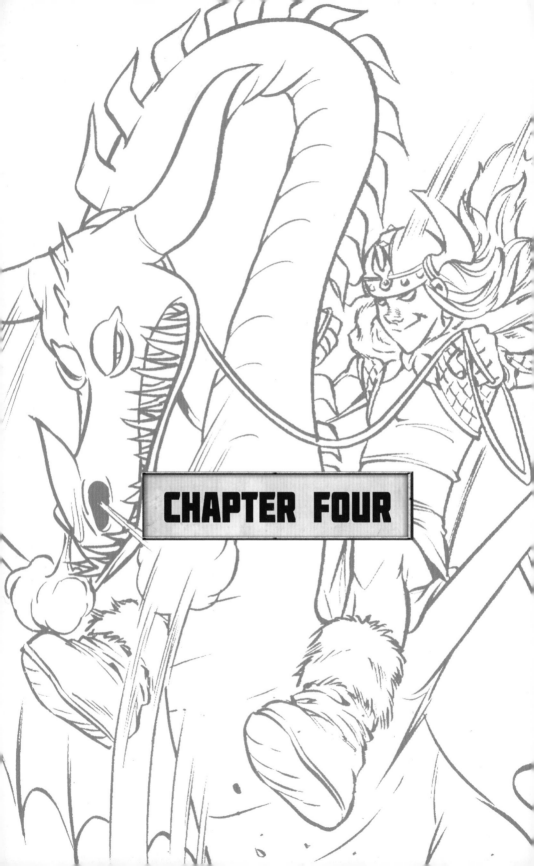

CHAPTER FOUR

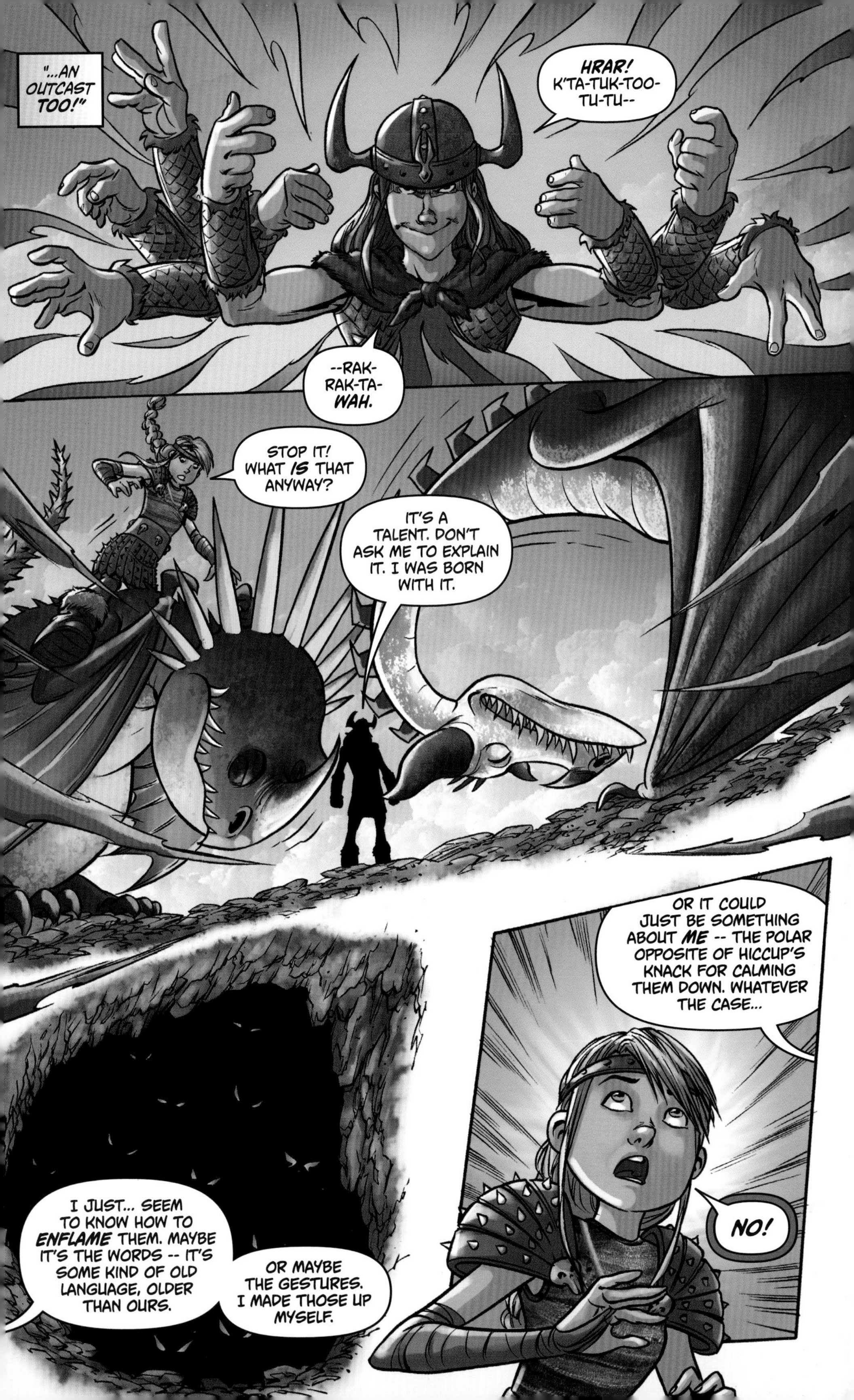

"...AN OUTCAST TOO!"
HRAR! K'TA-TUK-TOO-TU-TU--
--RAK-RAK-TA-WAH.
STOP IT! WHAT IS THAT ANYWAY?
IT'S A TALENT. DON'T ASK ME TO EXPLAIN IT. I WAS BORN WITH IT.
I JUST... SEEM TO KNOW HOW TO ENFLAME THEM. MAYBE IT'S THE WORDS -- IT'S SOME KIND OF OLD LANGUAGE, OLDER THAN OURS.
OR MAYBE THE GESTURES. I MADE THOSE UP MYSELF.
OR IT COULD JUST BE SOMETHING ABOUT ME -- THE POLAR OPPOSITE OF HICCUP'S KNACK FOR CALMING THEM DOWN. WHATEVER THE CASE...
NO!

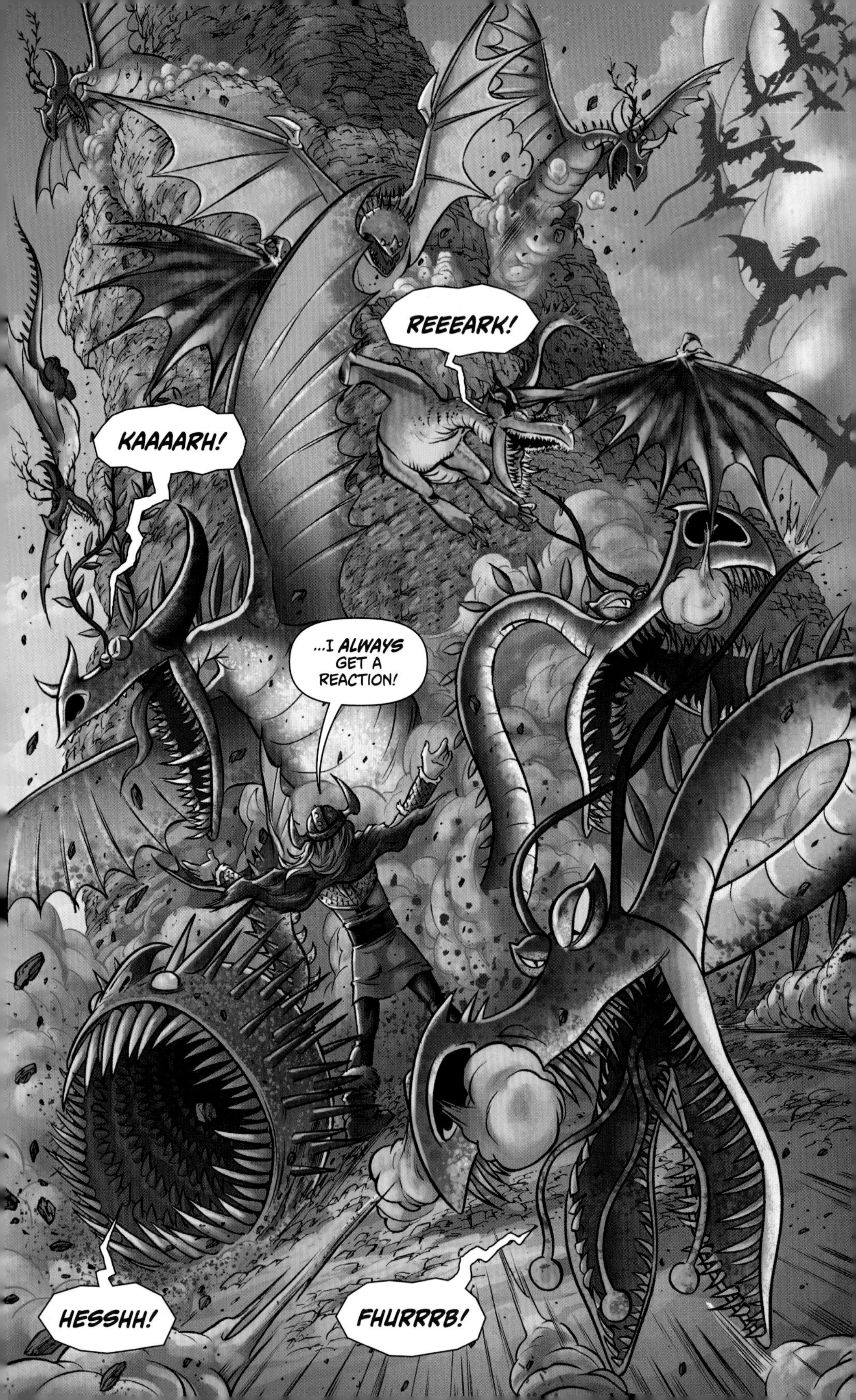
REEEARK!
KAAAARH!
...I ALWAYS GET A REACTION!
HESSHH!
FHURRRB!

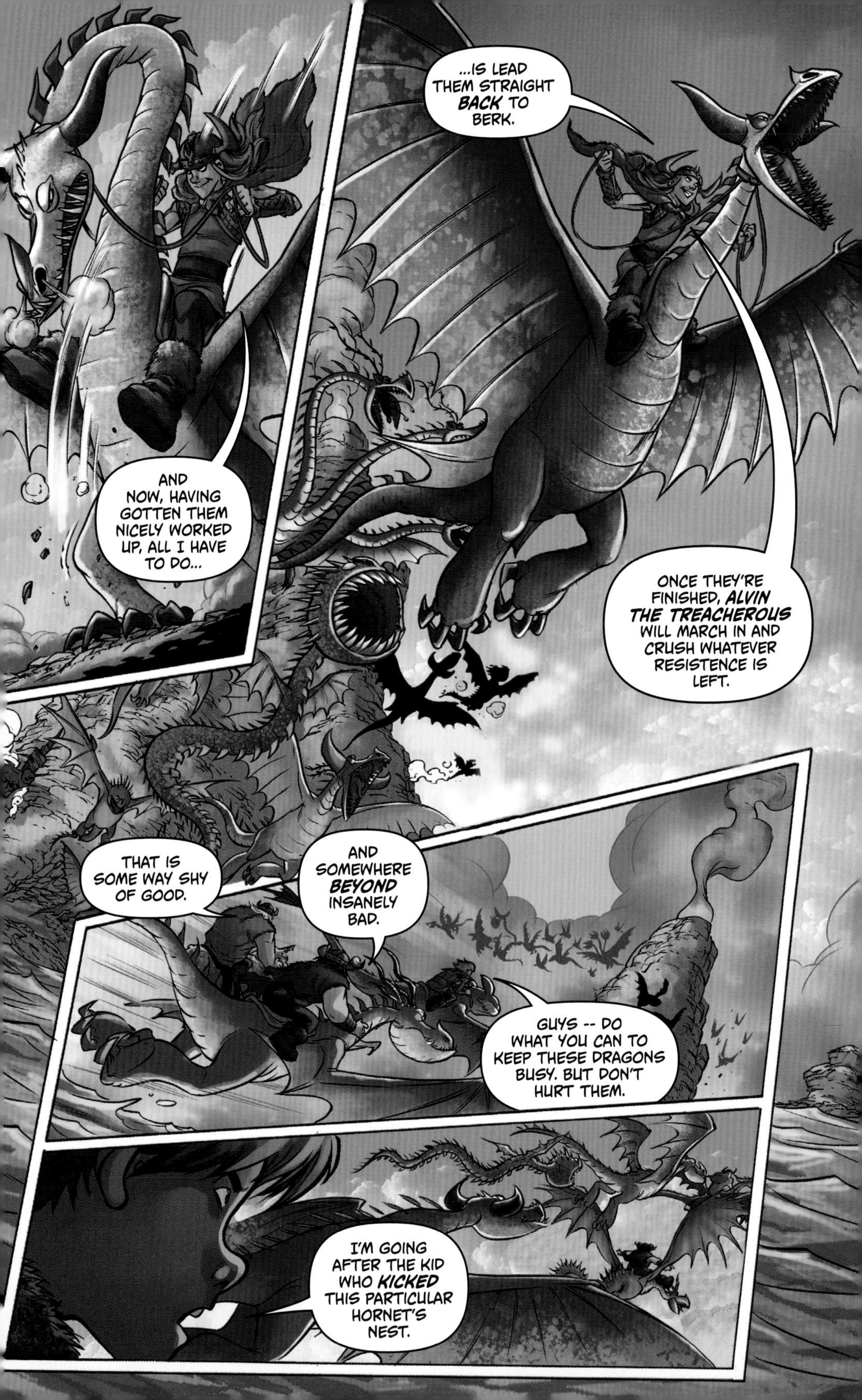
AND NOW, HAVING GOTTEN THEM NICELY WORKED UP, ALL I HAVE TO DO...
...IS LEAD THEM STRAIGHT BACK TO BERK.
ONCE THEY'RE FINISHED, ALVIN THE TREACHEROUS WILL MARCH IN AND CRUSH WHATEVER RESISTENCE IS LEFT.
THAT IS SOME WAY SHY OF GOOD.
AND SOMEWHERE BEYOND INSANELY BAD.
GUYS -- DO WHAT YOU CAN TO KEEP THESE DRAGONS BUSY. BUT DON'T HURT THEM.
I'M GOING AFTER THE KID WHO KICKED THIS PARTICULAR HORNET'S NEST.

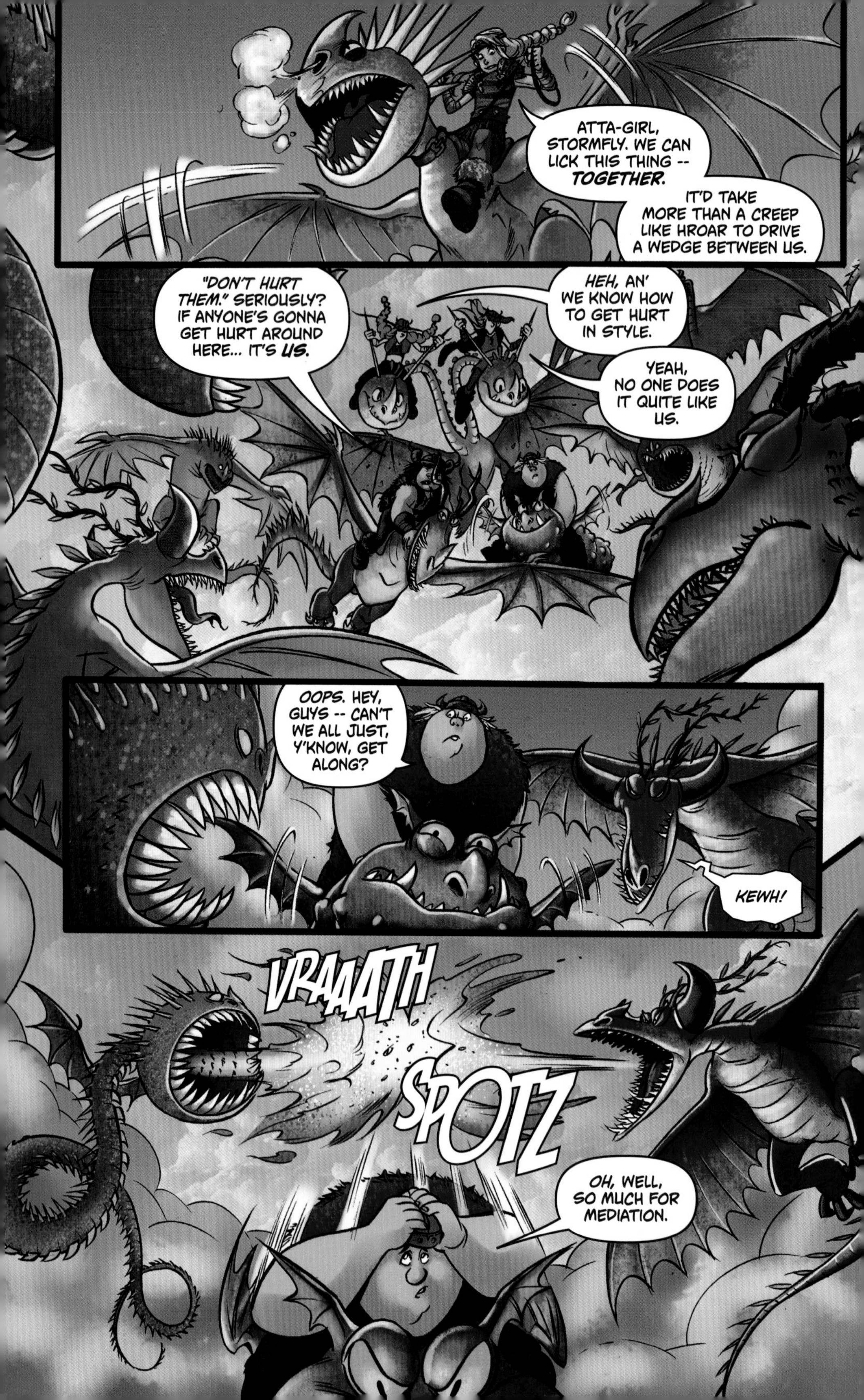

ATTA-GIRL, STORMFLY. WE CAN LICK THIS THING -- TOGETHER.
IT'D TAKE MORE THAN A CREEP LIKE HROAR TO DRIVE A WEDGE BETWEEN US.
"DON'T HURT THEM." SERIOUSLY? IF ANYONE'S GONNA GET HURT AROUND HERE... IT'S US.
HEH, AN' WE KNOW HOW TO GET HURT IN STYLE.
YEAH, NO ONE DOES IT QUITE LIKE US.
OOPS. HEY, GUYS -- CAN'T WE ALL JUST, Y'KNOW, GET ALONG?
KEWH!
VRAAATH
SPOTZ
OH, WELL, SO MUCH FOR MEDIATION.

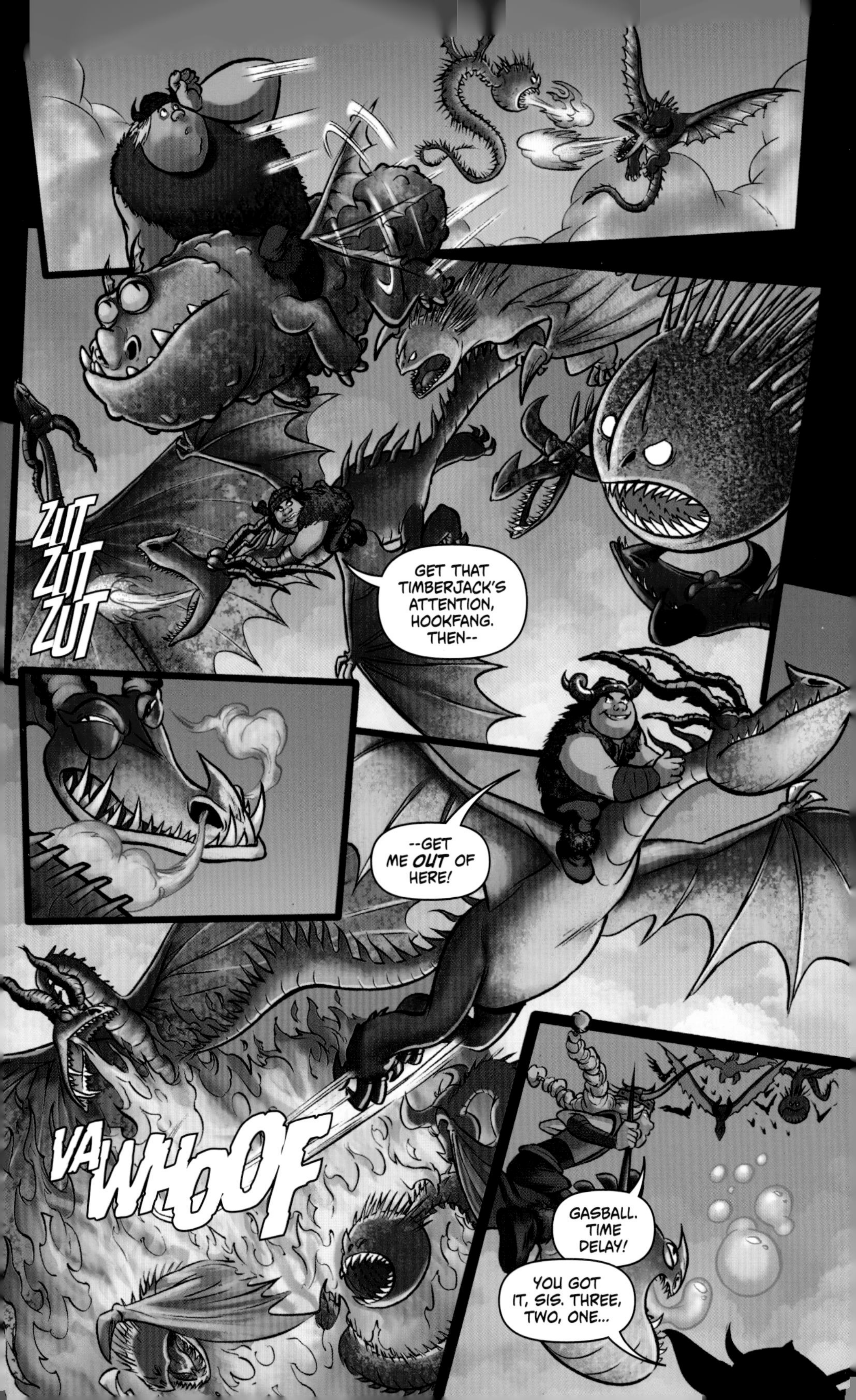
ZUT ZUT ZUT
GET THAT TIMBERJACK'S ATTENTION, HOOKFANG. THEN--
--GET ME OUT OF HERE!
VA WHOOF
GASBALL. TIME DELAY!
YOU GOT IT, SIS. THREE, TWO, ONE...

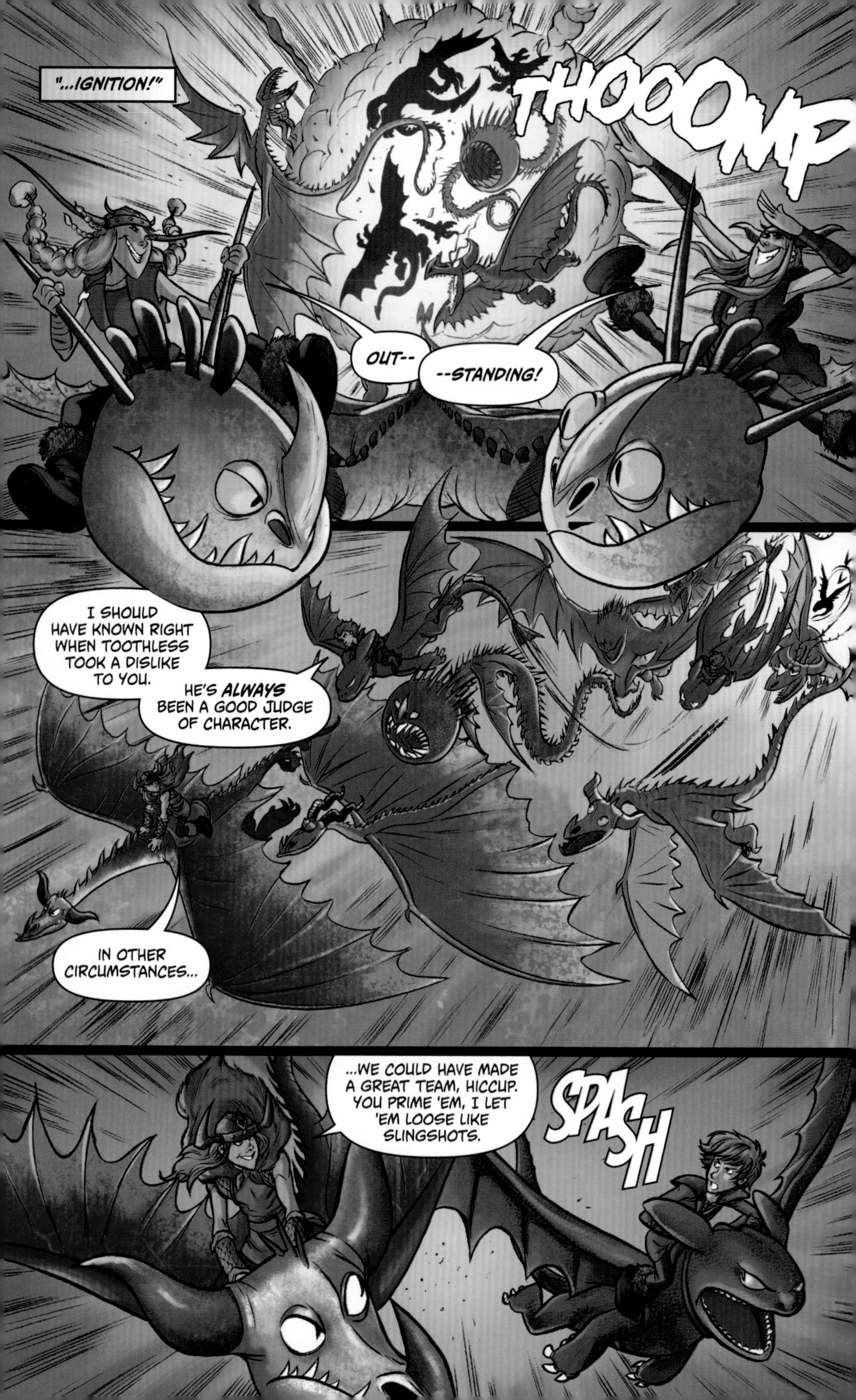
"...IGNITION!"
THOOOMP
OUT--
--STANDING!
I SHOULD HAVE KNOWN RIGHT WHEN TOOTHLESS TOOK A DISLIKE TO YOU.
HE'S ALWAYS BEEN A GOOD JUDGE OF CHARACTER.
IN OTHER CIRCUMSTANCES...
...WE COULD HAVE MADE A GREAT TEAM, HICCUP. YOU PRIME 'EM, I LET 'EM LOOSE LIKE SLINGSHOTS.
SPASH

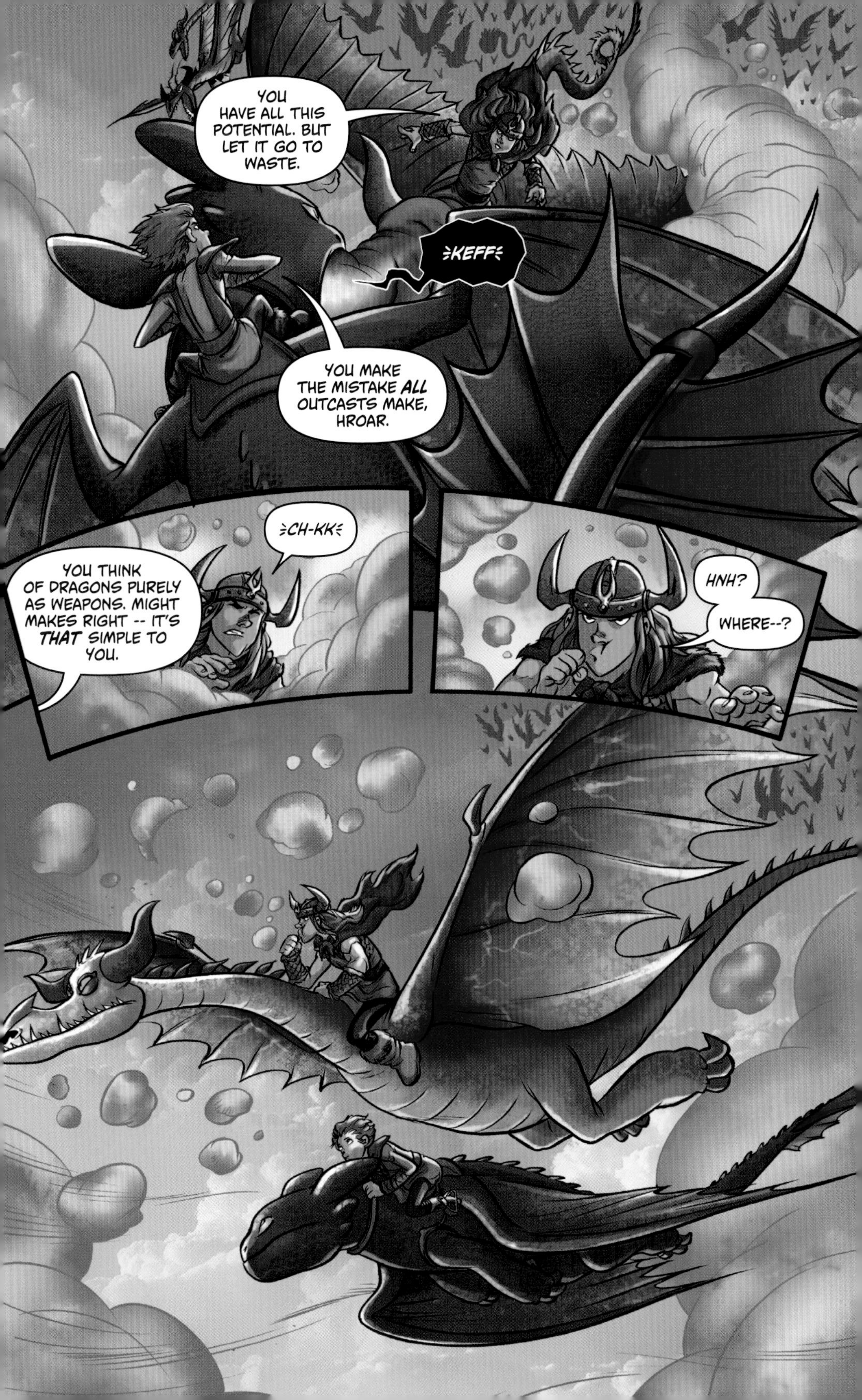
YOU HAVE ALL THIS POTENTIAL. BUT LET IT GO TO WASTE.
KEFF
YOU MAKE THE MISTAKE ALL OUTCASTS MAKE, HROAR.
CH-KK
YOU THINK OF DRAGONS PURELY AS WEAPONS. MIGHT MAKES RIGHT -- IT'S THAT SIMPLE TO YOU.
HNH?
WHERE--?

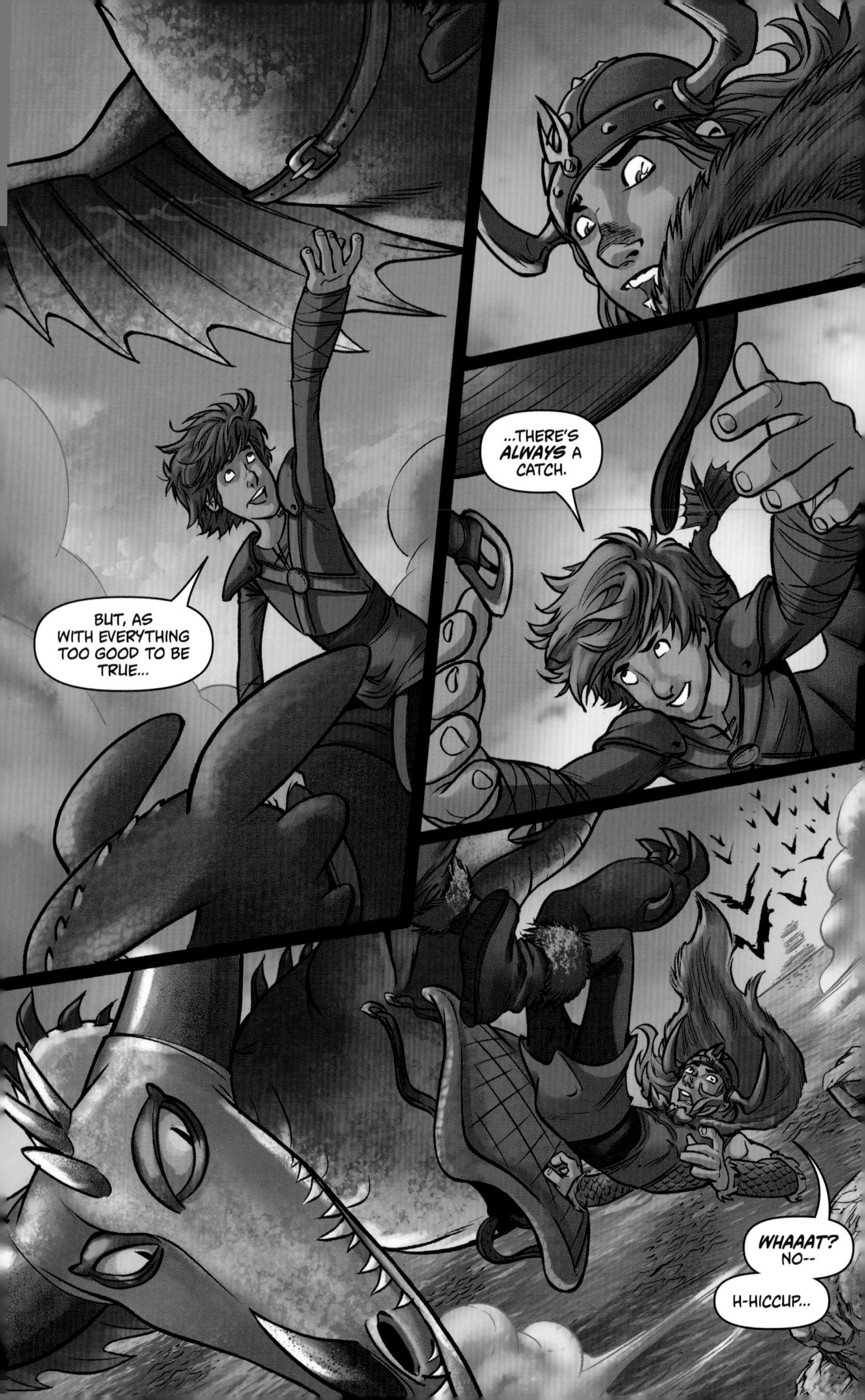
BUT, AS WITH EVERYTHING TOO GOOD TO BE TRUE...
...THERE'S *ALWAYS* A CATCH.
WHAAAT? NO--
H-HICCUP...

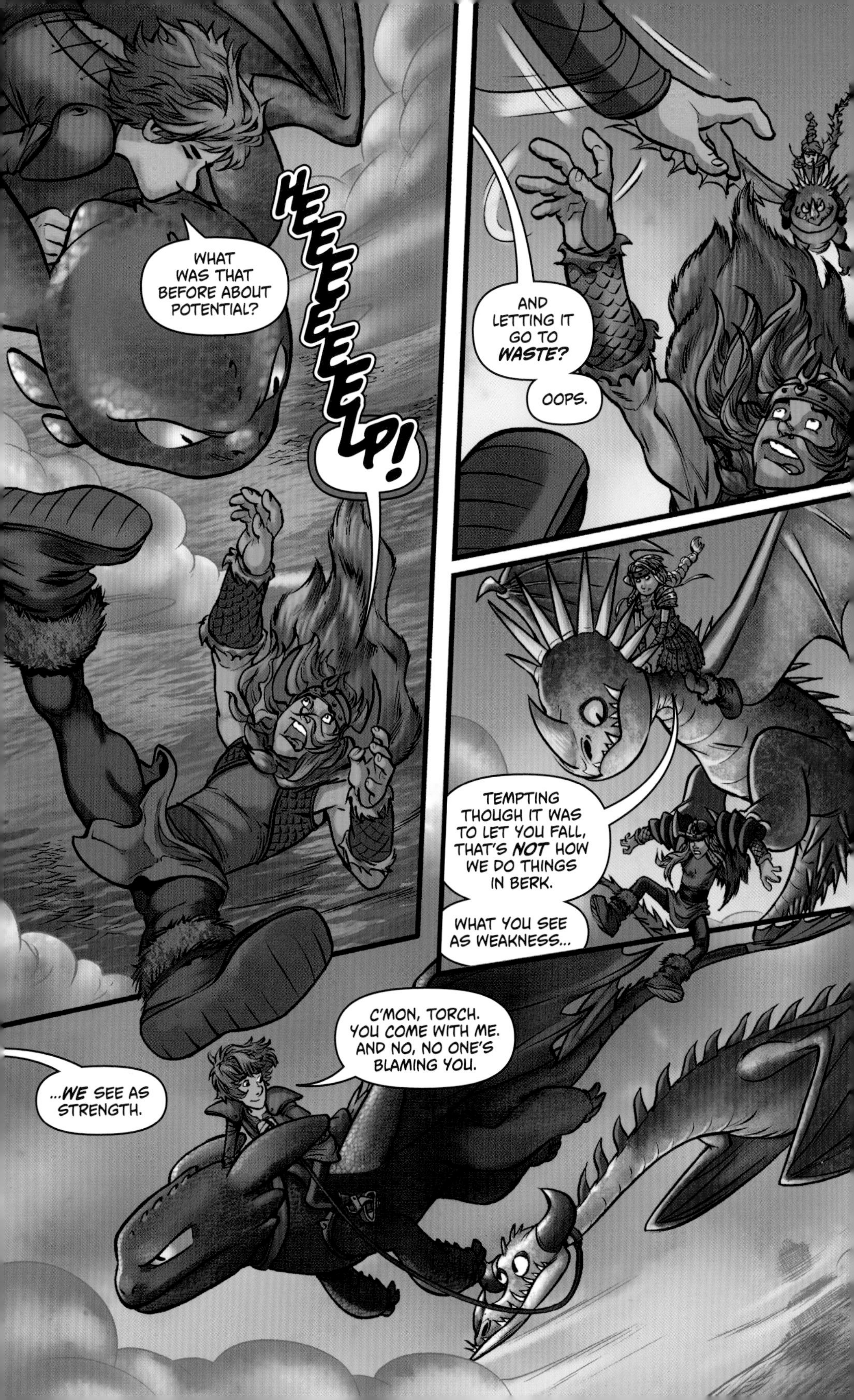
WHAT WAS THAT BEFORE ABOUT POTENTIAL?
HEEEEEEELP!
AND LETTING IT GO TO WASTE?
OOPS.
TEMPTING THOUGH IT WAS TO LET YOU FALL, THAT'S NOT HOW WE DO THINGS IN BERK.
WHAT YOU SEE AS WEAKNESS...
...WE SEE AS STRENGTH.
C'MON, TORCH. YOU COME WITH ME. AND NO, NO ONE'S BLAMING YOU.

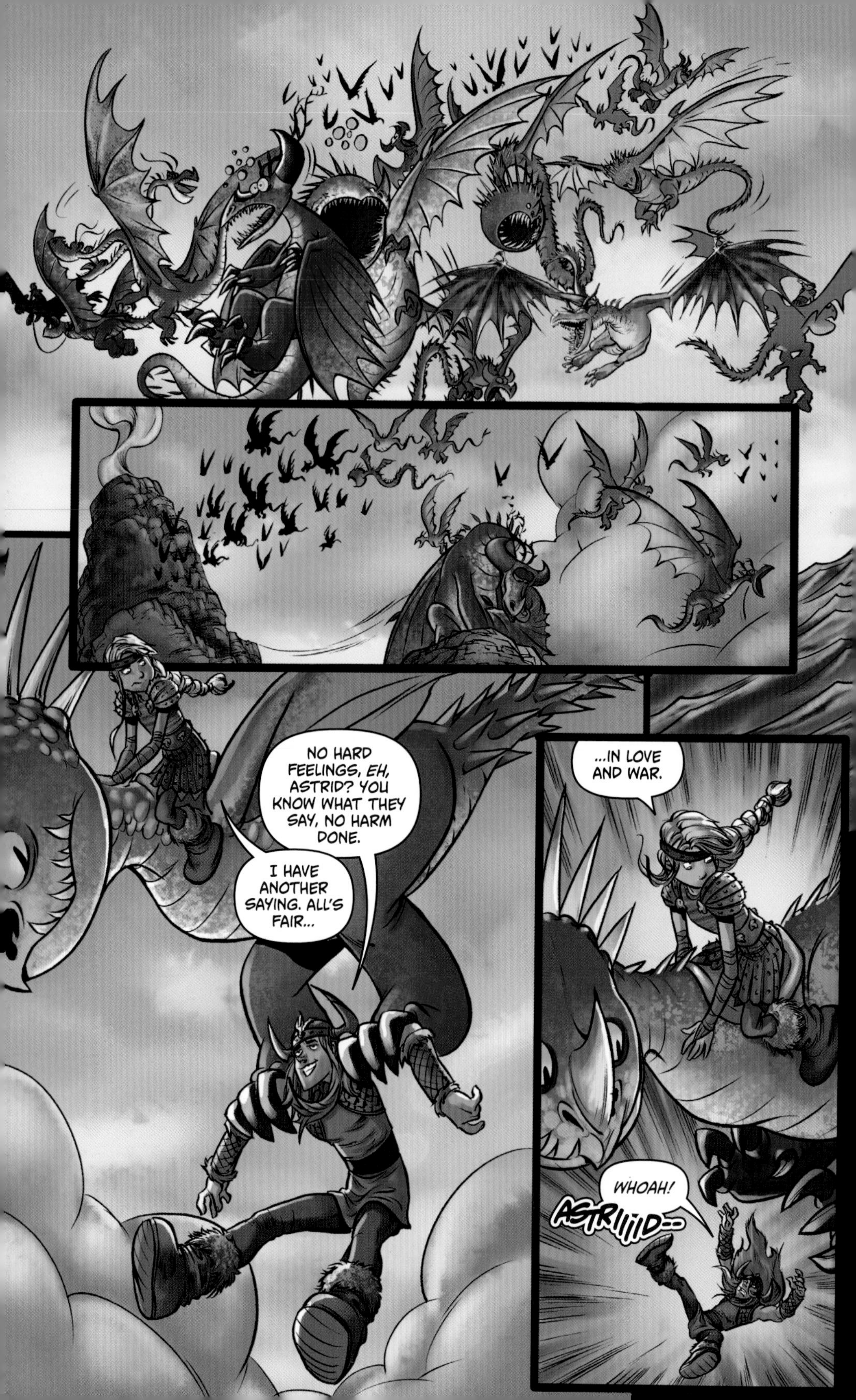
NO HARD FEELINGS, EH, ASTRID? YOU KNOW WHAT THEY SAY, NO HARM DONE.
I HAVE ANOTHER SAYING. ALL'S FAIR...
...IN LOVE AND WAR.
WHOAH!
ASTRIIIID--

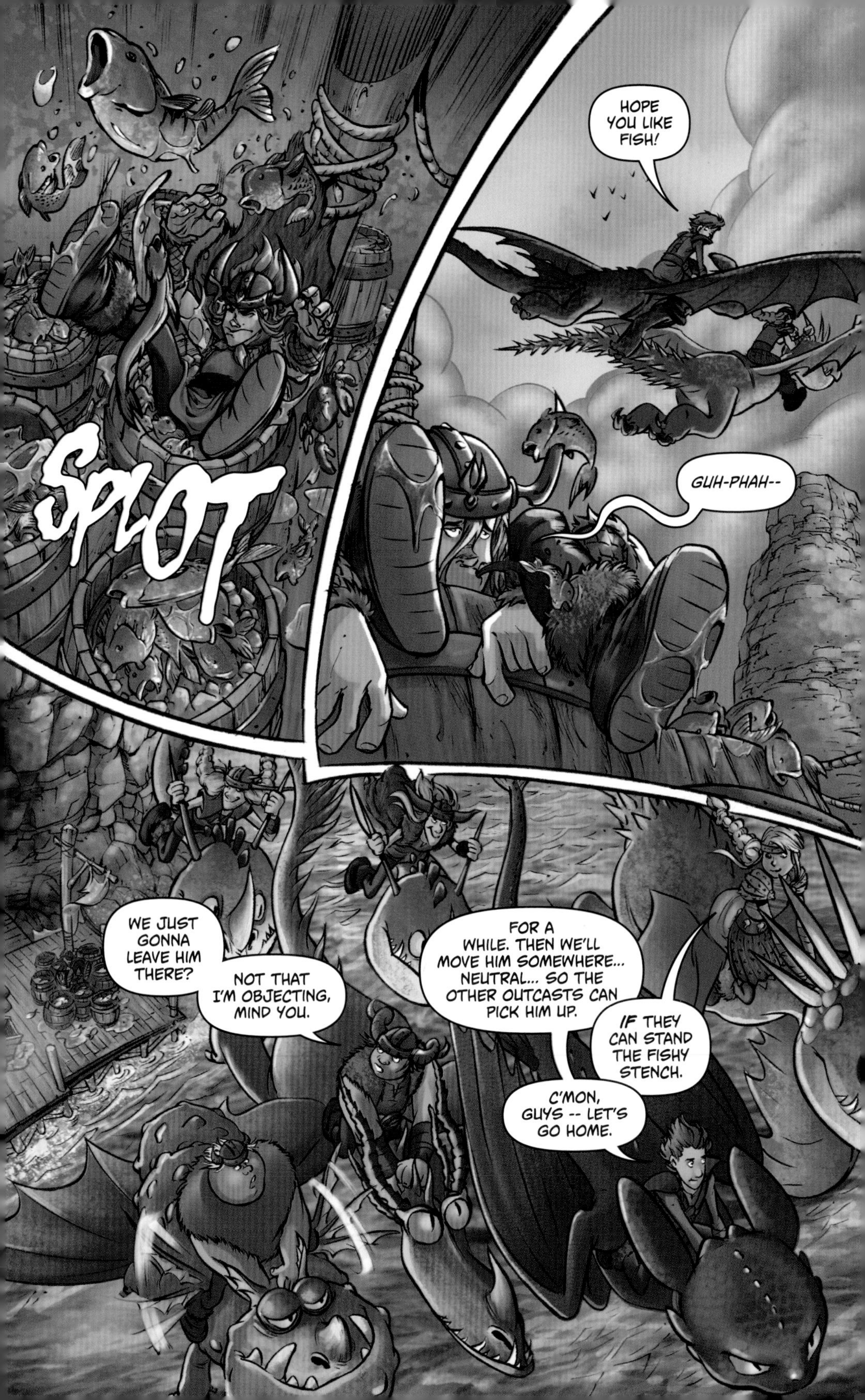
SPLOT
HOPE YOU LIKE FISH!
GUH-PHAH--
WE JUST GONNA LEAVE HIM THERE?
NOT THAT I'M OBJECTING, MIND YOU.
FOR A WHILE. THEN WE'LL MOVE HIM SOMEWHERE... NEUTRAL... SO THE OTHER OUTCASTS CAN PICK HIM UP.
IF THEY CAN STAND THE FISHY STENCH.
C'MON, GUYS -- LET'S GO HOME.

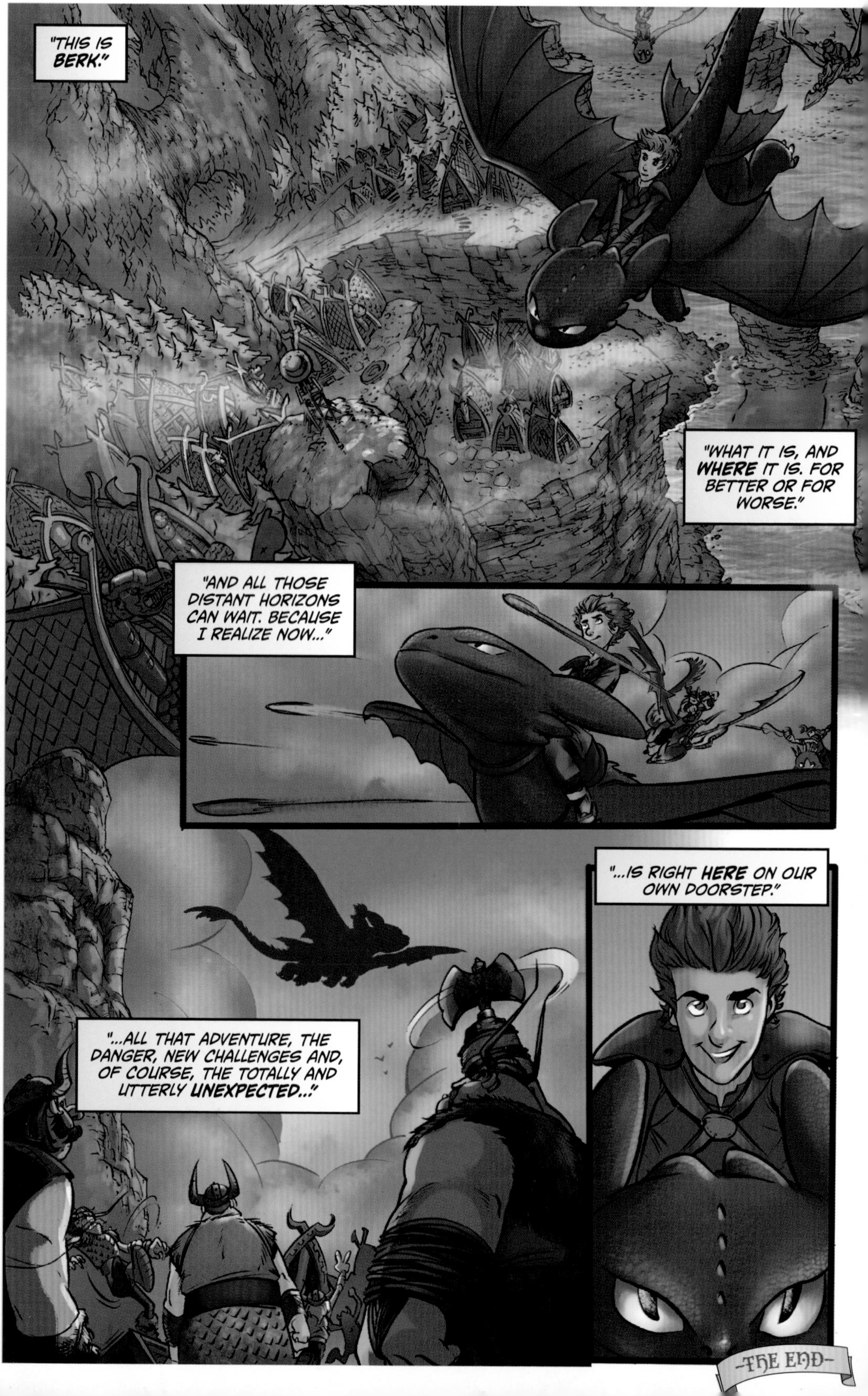
"THIS IS BERK."
"WHAT IT IS, AND WHERE IT IS. FOR BETTER OR FOR WORSE."
"AND ALL THOSE DISTANT HORIZONS CAN WAIT. BECAUSE I REALIZE NOW..."
"...ALL THAT ADVENTURE, THE DANGER, NEW CHALLENGES AND, OF COURSE, THE TOTALLY AND UTTERLY UNEXPECTED..."
"...IS RIGHT HERE ON OUR OWN DOORSTEP."
-THE END-

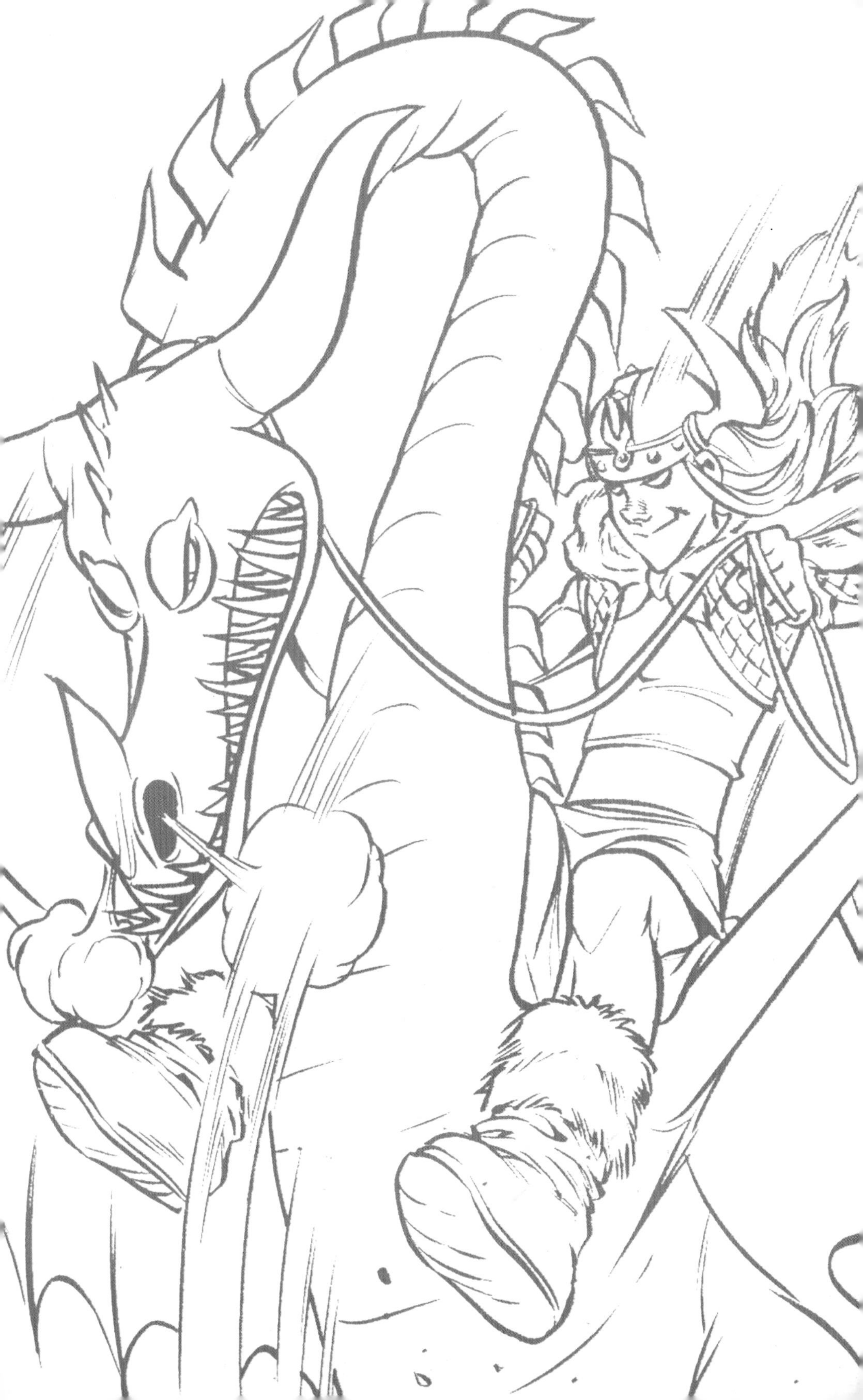

ON SALE NOW

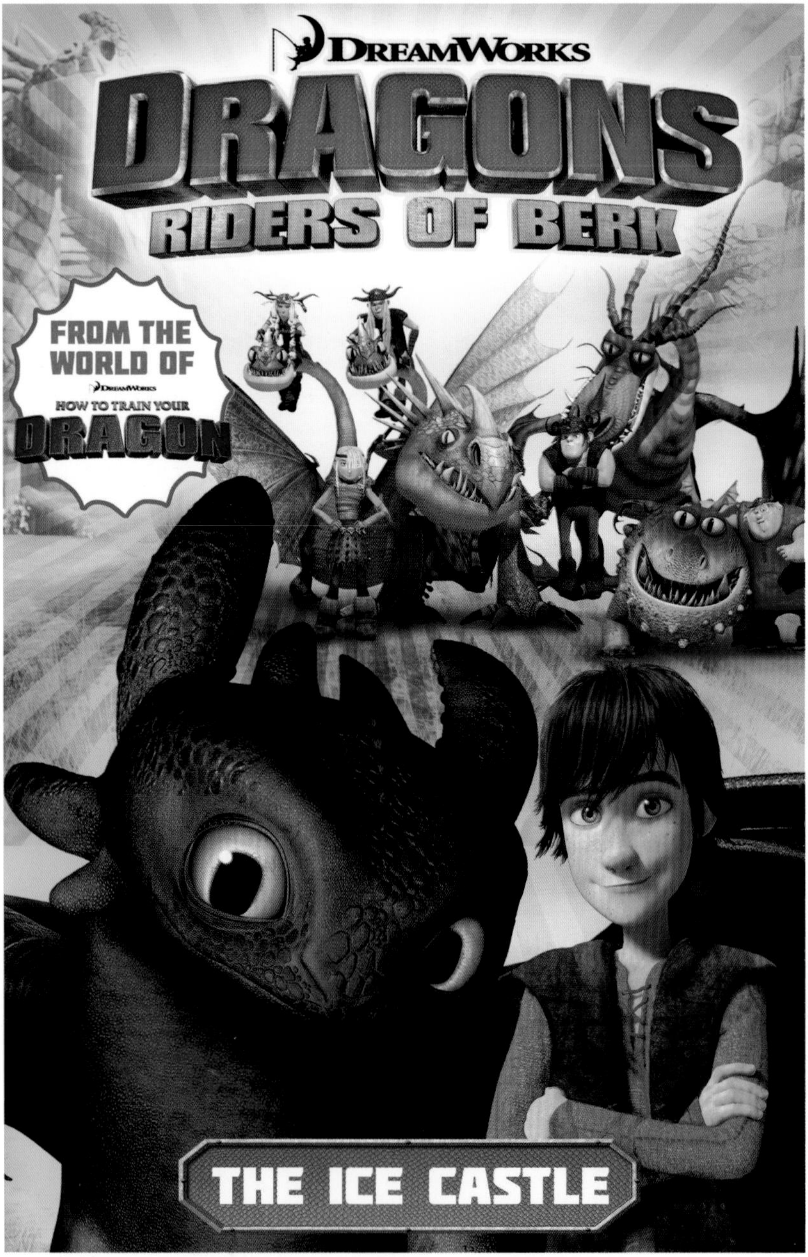
DREAMWORKS
DRAGONS
RIDERS OF BERK
FROM THE WORLD OF
DREAMWORKS
HOW TO TRAIN YOUR
DRAGON
THE ICE CASTLE

VOLUME THREE

Astrid's dragon, Stormfly, goes missing, and the whole of Berk tries to track her down! But what dangers will they ultimately face at... the Ice Castle? Plus, in a special short story, Snotlout babysits some infant Monstrous Nightmares!

OTHER VOLUMES

VOLUME ONE

Snotlout's dragon, Hookfang, flies off and goes missing, and a search party is organized... Unfortunately, Alvin the Treacherous is also on the hunt for Hookfang...
On sale now

VOLUME TWO

Berk is attacked while Hiccup is in charge... And in the scary Veil of Mists, Stoick and his crew are being stalked by something huge — and deadly...
On sale now

VOLUME FIVE

An ancient, deadly prophecy, a hypnotizing dragon, and Alvin the Treacherous all spell trouble...
Available May 5, 2015

VOLUME SIX

What will Hiccup and his friends discover in a mysterious dark pit? Plus, an old enemy returns...
Available July 7, 2015

For more information visit www.titan-comics.com